Pra...

'Tough, uncompromising voyage into the world of high-tech porn' *The Times*

'Part murder mystery, part erotic sci-fi fantasy . . . a *tour de force* by a writer of originality and imagination'
Hampstead & Highgate Express

'Shivery, original thriller; psychologically persuasive, technologically plausible – a health warning for all couch potatoes' *Literary Review*

'Just when I thought there were no new ideas in crime . . . an original and compelling story' *Million*

'. . . decidedly off-center and a refreshing antidote to the bland, well-trod ground covered so frequently in British whodunits' *San Francisco Examiner*

Denise Danks has been shortlisted twice for the CWA Gold Dagger, for *Phreak* and *Baby Love*, and has also been shortlisted for a Sherlock Award for Best Detective. She was recently described by *The Times* as one of the six best crime writers in the UK. *Frame Grabber* is her third novel featuring Georgina Powers.

By Denise Danks

FEATURING GEORGINA POWERS

The Pizza House Crash
Better Off Dead
Frame Grabber
Wink a Hopeful Eye
Phreak
Baby Love

OTHER NOVELS

Torso

FRAME GRABBER

Denise Danks

ORION

An Orion paperback

First published in Great Britain in 1992
by Constable & Company Ltd
This paperback edition published in 2002
by Orion Books Ltd,
Orion House, 5 Upper St Martin's Lane,
London WC2H 9EA

A CIP catalogue record for this book is available
from the British Library.

ISBN 0 75284 398 2

Typeset in Sabon by
Deltatype Ltd, Birkenhead, Merseyside

Printed and bound in Great Britain by
Clays Ltd, St Ives plc

For Gloria
the big-hearted one

My thanks to Peter Phillips, the Electric Studio Products Ltd; Simon Lam, Synoptics Ltd; Stu Firth, Ismic; John Forster, Silicon Graphics Ltd; Philip Baldwin, CIX; Simon Jamieson; Mike Penny and Regan Prevost, Penny and Evans Ltd (for the systems management); and my good friend, Peter White, who was a *real* help this time.

CHAPTER ONE

Richard Munroe jabbed a spade-shaped, nail-bitten finger on the dusty computer screen.

'Go on, then, there it is.'

'Where?' I said.

'Under "Bang". There.'

I tapped the keyboard and the screen displayed the title of the piece – 'Bang And Oh Such Fun' – in a rudimentary typeface, white on black. I groaned while Richard laughed, as he must have laughed every time he'd seen the damned thing. Two hazy figures began to work in horizontal mode in two positions: in and out. Richard laughed again and I killed the program.

I leaned back in my chair – or rather, Richard's lopsided chair – propped back from his neat but overloaded news editor's desk in the cluttered wasteland of *Technology Week*'s busy Soho office. I used to have my own decrepit desk and chair there. Now I worked for myself and the furniture was my own.

'Kids shouldn't be able to get hold of this stuff,' I said.

'Fifteen-year-old kids?' he said.

'No, eleven-year-old kids, eight-year-olds. Kids.'

'I didn't know you cared about kids.'

'Just because I haven't got any, it doesn't follow that I don't care what happens to them.'

'Oh, George. The maternal instinct. You do have it after all. I'm very encouraged.'

I tugged the dirty disk from its slot. 'Not at all,' I said. 'It's just that I'll have to live with the little bastards when they grow up, know what I mean?'

Richard shook his fingers, as if they'd been scorched, and laughed again, then looked at his watch. 'Coming for a drink lunchtime?'

'Sorry, I'm off to a conference.'

He frowned. 'Which one? Have we got someone going?'

'IPEX,' I said, trying to sound vague. Richard wasn't buying. He scanned his desk diary, drawing a finger down the page. As news editor, he'd have been in charge of distributing the jobs. The editor, Max Winter, used to do it when I worked there. Richard was cosier. There was more fear then but it was a long time ago and Max and I had an understanding now. We didn't talk to each other unless we absolutely had to.

'Oh, yes. Image processing. Diane Shine's doing the exhibition. She won't have time for the conference. Look, there might be something interesting there . . .'

The telephone on Richard's desk interrupted him, warbling from under some press releases. He scooped them away and tucked the receiver between his chin and shoulder, holding one hand up indicating that I should wait. I started for the door, making him grab for my arm. He pressed the secrecy button on the set.

'It's a Julie Wentworth. I forgot to tell you. She's phoned a couple of times,' he whispered, as if she could hear.

I shrugged. I didn't know the name.

'Want to take it?' he said.

I looked at my watch and started walking. 'Take a message,' I said, 'I'm late.'

'She says it's about your computer porn piece.'

'Byee!'

'Pick up what you can . . .'

He was calling to me but I was out of the door. I didn't want to make any promises for that day. I had to meet someone and go somewhere with him afterwards. I didn't want to work that afternoon. Not for Richard, anyway.

I knew it had been a mistake. Well, at least I knew now. Two months had passed and I still couldn't believe that I had done it. It was incredible. I had had one or two drinks. I had loosened up, yes, but it was nothing I couldn't handle. But I had done it. I had had sex with an interviewee, the first time ever in a ten-year career in journalism. Right there, in a pastel-coloured hotel room on the twentieth floor of a monumental glass tower, at three o'clock in the afternoon.

We did it looking out over the Hudson River, with the hot breeze sucked up from the humid, New York streets rushing against my face. It was possible to see us through the huge tinted window, yet no one could. No one was watching us up there. But there was no 'we' or 'us', really. There was just me and him, separate pieces in the same pie. It was a very lonely business.

I had flown to New York for the launch of a new high-powered computer and Dr David Jones was one of many accompanying sideshows set up to illustrate the potential of the new system. His expertise? Computer-generated virtual reality: a technology that creates three-dimensional electronic worlds, computer models that you can exist in and interact with. Computer models that can be any world you want, with you as the chief inhabitant, but you don't have to be alone. I had to interview him for *Technology Week*, find out about his company, Virtech – a sexy little start-up, Richard had called it.

For just over an hour, we'd sat facing each other discussing what I thought were the relevant issues. I wasn't convinced that what I was hearing wasn't a load of hype so I decided to wind up on a light note.

'Do you remember those special-effect disaster movies?' I said.

'I'm afraid I don't,' he replied.

'*Earthquake*? You didn't see that?'

'No. I rarely see films, I prefer to make my own.'

'Really? Well, this should interest you. You could actually feel the tremors as they happened onscreen. Virtual reality isn't new, you see.'

'No, it isn't. The difference is that what you had was, essentially, a passive experience.'

'I felt something though, from a place I wasn't in. It was an illusion. The impact of your virtual world is also illusory. You can affect things, and effect them, but how much can they affect you?'

He leaned forward and placed his empty coffee cup next to my gently bubbling gin and tonic. He didn't drink on duty, and he didn't smoke, but the glass ashtray on the table was crammed with broken unburned matchsticks, some in bent chevrons and others snapped in two. One fresh splinter was hanging over the edge. He picked it up and gently clamped his teeth on one end, chewing slowly at it and twisting it around with his fingers. He kept his eyes on me for so long that I began to feel uncomfortable. I pushed the skirt of my loose dress down a little and reached for my tumbler of gin. I threw my head back to drink and I could see him through the bottom of the glass, staring at my neck and the low scoop of my summer dress.

'Did you enjoy it?' he said.

'The film?'

'The passive experience.'

'I don't remember. I think I screamed. It was fun.'

'A real earthquake isn't fun.'

'I know that. I bought a ticket, remember? I felt the quake, all the same.'

'And touched it?'

4

'Feel is not the same as touch.'

'It can be,' he said.

I looked over my glass, unable to put it down. I wanted to finish it but he prevented me somehow, holding my gaze long enough to make me look away for my cigarettes.

'Ask the military. We don't need to know everything in order to relate to something, just a few things with certainty,' he said.

'Like the sound and direction of an incoming bomb?' I said, relieved. Hypothetical weaponry was easier to handle than an intimate thought.

'Quite.'

'But not the smell or the taste of burning.'

'No.'

'Without the smell or taste of burning how do we understand the danger of the bomb?' I said.

'Instinct,' he said. 'Pure instinct.'

He sat back in his pale pink chair, both hands casually resting on his thighs, his legs slightly splayed, and the light caught his glasses enough to white out his eyes. In a moment, the reflection of the sky had gone and I noticed his pale blue eyes were very steady, as if he had me in his sights. I put my glass down and folded my notebook, slotting my pencil through the spiral at the top. He'd ordered more drinks a while back, but I decided it was time to go. I looked up to say so and he smiled a little. His eyes were alight and I knew he was back on track.

'Everyone wants it, everyone,' he said.

'And why's that?'

'Because everybody can think of at least one thing they'd like to do with it.'

There was a knock on the door before I could reply. A young black man, trim in his green uniform with shiny brass buttons, entered with our third and final tray of drinks. When he'd gone, I raised my glass to my companion but as I lifted it up to drink, the ice clung to the bottom and then slid down, banging my lip. I pressed a napkin to my face and dabbed a drip or two off my chin and the thin material of my dress. I looked up and David shifted his glasses on his face as ice water trickled down my belly.

'Mind if I smoke?' I said, laying the damp napkin over the arm of my chair. I stuck an unlit cigarette in my mouth.

'What would you like to do?' he said.

'Me? Nothing.'

'You could do whatever you wanted.'

'I do now.'

'Without suffering the consequences.'

That last statement was going to play on my mind. I'd never got away with anything, never ever. If I didn't pick up the whole bill, I got to pay more than a few instalments. He was looking at me for some sort of reaction. I didn't give it. I didn't light my cigarette either. I took it out of my mouth and he handed me a box of matches.

'Did you get to play?' he said.

'Downstairs? No. There was a queue. The boys got there first.'

'In that case, you can ride my machine,' he said.

That surprised me. His voice betrayed the innuendo but he didn't look like the sort of man that would make one. He wasn't the sort of man who was unaware of what he said either. I played it straight.

'Thank you. Tell me, is your reality more real than theirs?' I said.

'Of course it is. It's more expensive. VR is about affecting perceptions. You can do this with simple equipment and relatively unsophisticated graphics because the human sensory system is remarkably tolerant to pathetically sparse audiovisual stimulation. For more

6

realism you need a system that can solve extensive sets of equations at speed. You need processors working in parallel. The more you need, the more you have to pay. Reality costs.'

I still hadn't lit the cigarette. It was stuck to my lip. He leaned over, gently took the wooden matchbox from my hands and stroked a match along the side. It crackled and flared and I sucked in the flame, keeping myself from looking up until I needed to puff smoke into the air. It was time to smack his wrists.

'All right. Conceptually, it sounds very different, but what are we really talking about here? A sophisticated display with interesting peripherals, that's all, a pretentious box,' I said.

He picked a fresh match from the box, snapped it till it almost broke, put one end in his mouth and flicked the other with his thumb so that it twirled around. I took a few triumphant puffs of my cigarette until he flicked the twisted match into the ashtray with the others and got up, gesturing to the window. He waited by the table for me and guided me towards it, one hand pressing the cotton of my dress against the small of my back.

The window stretched from one wall to the other. There was the wide, grey Hudson River and the wake of a cargo ship curved round the distant bulk of the Statue of Liberty. I imagined the river to be noisy with traffic, but we couldn't hear it. I could hear him breathing softly. He tapped the thick, smoky glass with his knuckle.

'Think of this as the screen. All that you see would be digitized, within the computer. And you? You could be what you want, do what you want. You could be a bird or a plane. Alice through the Looking Glass. Look, over there. You could be Liberty. Reach down and drag your fingers through the water. Push the clouds wide apart.'

I stared ahead, peering through the glass until all I could see was his reflection. He was slightly taller than me and as spare. His white shirt had the sleeves rolled up to expose intermittent fair hairs on his lightly tanned arm. I could see he wasn't looking at the view, imagining what he could be. He was looking at me.

'Look, I feel a bit cold,' I said, trying to turn.

He looked back to where the dials were fixed to the opposite wall. 'I could regulate the air conditioning . . .' he replied. 'Or . . .'

His arm moved over my shoulder and he tugged hard at the handle, swinging the huge window before us open a couple of inches. The hot summer wind whistled in over my face and down my body. It puffed out my thin dress and shook my dark hair. He took one strand from his lip and put both hands gently on my shoulders. We stood unbearably close together, looking out across the grey water, listening to the breeze until he took my wrists tightly and placed my hands a little above my head, palms flat against the thick glass.

'Look out. You can see everything except what is directly below. Now look down. See? It's a long way, isn't it? You could be flying, imagine that, up and down, in and out . . . why don't you do it, now?' he said.

He was pushing against me so my hips pressed against the sill. I caught my breath as my eyes took in the giddying, twenty-floor drop. There was no glass before me, just air. I could see little coloured cars like kiddies' bricks on the street. My fingers pressed hard and flat against the glass like a lizard's on a high, dry wall. He tugged the skirt of my dress and twined the hem around and around his fingers until it tightened around my thighs. He pulled it up slowly, dragging it over my cotton-knickered hips, up to my waist. His other hand held the back of my neck, while he pulled the pants down, and the dress up higher to expose my naked breasts. We were standing right in front of the window, where nothing but the birds could see us. He kneaded my

8

flesh in his hands and my legs trembled against his while my brain worked desperately to stabilize the distance from the ground up and find the word – no.

The sudden, hard pressure behind crushed my stomach against the wood and metal of the window sill. All that seemed to keep me on solid ground were the tips of my sandalled toes. My face slid uncomfortably against the glass between my outspread arms. He pulled me back, held my neck again, squeezing tightly, pressing down on the bones of my spine, keeping my face against the dry wind and above the drop. The distant street below began to judder back and forth until I shut my eyes tight. I felt as if I were flying blind on a warm, red edge, swelling and thickening like a thermistor in a tight vial, my voice nothing but an idiot's hum locked in my head. He quickened with my heartbeat and with the final push came a short sigh and a rough shove against my shoulders. My weight jerked the window violently outwards and my eyes stretched open in shock as I tumbled forward and down.

The street came towards me fast. I had an idea that I was screaming as the hot air blasted with renewed force against my face. I could hear nothing, nothing but the increased roar of the wind drying the moisture from my tongue and teeth. I was falling, alone and afraid of falling, falling all the way to the ground. A shaft of ecstasy and a pinching sensation of fear prickled up through me like boiling sand, spilling over my scalp like needled splinters. I shuddered against the impact which never came. I had gone nowhere. I stood leaning against the window, gasping and staring downwards. All was still, but for the little coloured bricks stopping and starting, whizzing and braking, way down on the street.

Two more inches. The window had moved out two more inches, that's all. It had seemed like two feet, maybe a metre. The hotels fix them like that. The gap has to be

9

too small to drop a TV set or your head through. Two inches or two feet, I was shaking as if I had truly been snatched back from the sky.

By the time I turned around, he had already straightened his clothes. He looked neat and calm, as if he had just walked into the room. I pulled my dress down and went to the bathroom. To be sick, I thought, but all I did was smooth my dress against me and flick at my hair before leaving the suite. There was someone in the corridor waiting for his interview. I heard David say, in his polite, English way, 'Good afternoon. Sorry to have kept you.'

Just like he had said to me.

CHAPTER TWO

I got to the exhibition five minutes late but David wasn't waiting. I felt an ache of disappointment in my chest. He hadn't turned up. Or he'd turned up and gone. My heart was beating hard from the effort of the journey and anticipation. I moved from one spot to another by the busy cloakroom watching businessmen in lightweight suits, dishevelled by the heat, push through the heavy glass and metal doors into the foyer to check in. I was only five minutes late. I looked around again, at the check-in desk, to be sure, then at the second set of doors that led to the exhibition hall, then back to the main doors. He was always on time. I was usually early. He was always on time. He had said to stand by the cloakroom. I'd done that. I was doing that, but I was five minutes late. I began to panic. Was there more than one cloakroom? I turned to ask and my bag slithered from my shoulder on to the floor. Matchsticks, broken matchsticks. Some chevrons, some snapped in two, scattered around like birds' feet.

I looked up and saw him, a still figure in the bustle of people. He stood directly opposite me, to one side of the lift, in one of the thickly carpeted corridors that led away to the left and right of the hall. With one hooked finger, he held the jacket of his suit over his shoulder. His dark tie was neatly tied, fixed with a diamond pin, and the collar of his white shirt buttoned. He looked cool and unruffled while I felt the perspiration trickle down between my breasts.

'David, I'm sorry,' I said, stepping near him.

'I have to give my presentation in ten minutes.'

'Where were you?'

'Here.'

'All the time?'

'I haven't got all day. I've booked a room.'

He passed a yellow memo slip to me. On it he'd written a room number and the name of a hotel two streets away. It was a big, plush hotel. David liked big, plush rooms when he was in town. I lived in town, but he never came to my home. He said it wasn't convenient.

'How long are you staying?'

'Never mind that. Come with me,' he said.

I followed him down the silent corridor, hurrying behind him along a red and mauve carpet that extended right up the walls to the ceiling where a myriad tiny spotlights dropped light shafts in the gloom. He led me quickly up two flights of stairs away from the noise of the foyer and the busy chatter in the huge hall. The corridor was unlit here and to the right was a large, empty cloakroom with row upon row of chained metal hangers extending back into utter blackness. He stepped in behind the counter and waited by the first row. I hesitated for just a moment and then walked towards him, the hairs on my scalp rising like soldiers from the dead as I turned into the dark.

Diane Shine, one of *Technology Week*'s young reporters, was about to leave the IPEX press office as I walked in.

'Oh hi, Georgina. Richard called, says you're covering the conference for us. That's OK. Helps me out . . .' She stopped and peered into my face. 'Are you OK?'

I looked around at the sheaves of press releases lining the walls just to stop her looking into my eyes.

'Gasping for a drink.'

'Oh, there's coffee over there and a few sandwiches . . .' She nodded to the formica table bearing trays of cups, coffee and sandwiches.

I shook my head. 'A drink . . . as in Gordon's, Jamieson's, Black Label, as in pie, pint and a few kind words . . .'

Diane's pretty, dolly eyes scrunched up in a mockery of pain and she bent down to run a smooth finger around the back of one flat, pointed shoe. 'Wouldn't mind one myself, actually. I hate trekking around these exhibitions. My bleeding feet,' she said.

We walked together to the far end of the exhibition where the bar was less crowded than the others. I hadn't really wanted company. What I really needed was a couple of quick, lonely shots. The fear had gone. I was angry now. How do I manage it, I asked myself. How do I manage to pick up these bastards?

'Here, this one's on Max,' Diane said, shoving the drink along the bar to me. I took a swallow. It was cold and bitter. Cold. Cold as he was. And bitter? No, not enough feeling for bitterness. Diane nodded at my chest and I looked down.

'Your buttons are done up wrong.'

So they were, and the skin across my back itched.

'Oh, before I forget, here . . . Richard said to call her back. It's about your porn story . . .' she said as I straightened my blouse. She passed me a piece of paper torn from her notebook. The name 'Julie Wentworth' and a number were scrawled across the paper in Diane's large, expansive script. 'Good story. The tabloids certainly picked up on that, didn't they? Bet Max was pleased we had it first.'

'He didn't. He just thought he did,' I said, tucking the paper into my bag, catching sight of David's memo as I did so. I drained my glass and leaned around a hefty, male shoulder with perspiring armpit to catch the attention of the barmaid. Diane chattered on.

'Glad we don't have much to do with him.'

'Who?'

'Max.'

'Mmm.'

'Now Richard's different. I like Richard. He's rather sweet, isn't he just?'

'I'm sure he'd love to hear you say so,' I said.

Diane leaned her brown arm on the bar, resting her rounded little chin in her palm. 'He's so sort of . . . you know . . . sexy.'

'From Pooh Bear to Richard Gere is an enormous leap, Diane.'

She laughed into her drink and the barmaid started towards me. I ordered a double. Diane shook her head and stuck to a single. Then we sat back on tall chrome and sticky vinyl stools, surveying the drinks and then the bar. Wall to wall men and none like David. He had to be one in a . . . million? No, he was rarer than that. I took a long swallow. I hoped he was.

Diane jabbed a long finger into her drink, rattling the fast-melting ice. 'Georgina . . .'

'Ye . . . es.'

'Do you approve of affairs at work?'

'They're OK until you fall out.'

'Voice of experience?'

'Vicarious experience.'

'Oh, I believe you.'

'Believe me. I've always been far too busy screwing up relationships elsewhere.'

Diane jabbed her ice cubes again. They bobbed up persistently. 'You know what?'

'What?'

'You won't laugh?'

I pulled a face, the one I thought she could trust, and

14

did the old dib dib Girl Guide routine. That seemed to satisfy her. She sucked up an ice cube and rolled it slowly around her mouth. A couple of seconds later, it popped from between her pomegranate lips and dropped back into the glass with a plop.

'I fancy Richard,' she said. I choked and she walloped my shoulder. 'It's true. I actually dream about him.'

'Well, Diane, dreaming of Richard would certainly send me to sleep,' I said, tapping a cigarette out of its packet. I offered her one. She shook her head. I lit up and puffed a cylinder of smoke straight upwards. There were fewer complaints that way.

'Familiarity breeds contempt, does it?'

'Just narcolepsy.'

'You cow.'

I pointed at an ashtray. She asked the man next to her for it and he passed it over, all smiles. She gave him a real treat and smiled back.

'I'm serious,' she said.

'You mean, you fantasize about him. Don't try and tell me you dream. That's involuntary.'

Diane thought about this. 'I do both,' she said.

'You're crazy.'

'He's got nice gentle eyes.'

'They're wet.'

'He's got lovely big hands.'

'He bites his fingernails.'

'He's mature.'

'He's losing his hair.'

'Oh yeah, but nicely, you know, from the front.'

'Gawd.'

She must have been the only person alive to fantasize about my landlord Richard but I bet he fantasized about her all right. Every hetero male in the office did. Maybe even that cold fish, Max, wondered about Diane Shine and her lovely, high, round breasts. I couldn't be sure of the females, of course, but why not? She had long, dark legs that crept up her tight skirt to a waist you could put two hands around and touch fingertips. She was neat but not prim. She smiled a lot, and when she did her even teeth shone white and bright against her smooth dark skin. Richard, however, had a chewed-up slipper sort of look. His rugby-playing days were behind him and, as a result, his stomach was beginning to spread in front. His eyes were nice, though. She was right. He had kind eyes, soft brown with thick, dark lashes.

David's eyes were always pale and closed off. He kept his glasses on when we made love. After all, we never kissed. It was so lonely being close to Dr David Jones. But I turned up whenever he called. Whenever he was in town, I always came running, alive with terrible longing, and dread.

This time he hadn't taken my clothes off. I had, because he told me to. He didn't even undo his collar. I could hardly see him but I could feel him, not touch him, feel him. He stood close to me in the darkness, crowding me as I undid my buttons and slipped off my clothes as quickly as my anxious fingers allowed. When I tried to speak, he covered my mouth with his hand. It was neither warm nor cold. Dry and smooth. I stood there, white as a bone in the dark corner, with an ache in my crotch and a sick thrill in my stomach as he edged closer to me. His shoulders and then his body crushed me against the carpeted corner so that every little, itchy fibre dug into my back. He leaned against me with all his weight, so that I felt the knot of his tie, the diamond pin, his hard belt buckle on my belly. He pushed harder and harder, for longer and longer, until the breath was squeezed from my lungs and I couldn't expand my chest to breathe in. My arms thrashed at his back until he pulled away and the air rushed into my lungs like water in a flash flood. I sat alone among my crumpled clothes, breathing hard, in and out, in and out. He had gone.

'Hey.' It was Diane's voice. 'Hey, your hand's shaking.'

I looked down at the glass. My fingers were trembling against it. I pulled my hand back and rubbed my elbow. 'Must have leaned on a nerve,' I said. I would be damned if I'd meet him now.

'You're right,' said Diane, finally, draining her drink.

'What?'

'About Richard. Beware of what you wish for, as mama used to say.'

'Yeah. Good old mama.'

'Heaven forbid, if some of our fantasies came to life, eh? I mean, no vicar would be safe, would he?' She patted me on the back before swinging her long legs around and on to the floor. 'Thanks for the drink. I gave you that note, didn't I?' she said, beginning to open her bag again.

I stopped her and waved goodbye in her face. She grinned. I grinned back until she'd gone and I turned back to the bar. I needed another drink, or two, and a cigarette.

The room key in reception was gone, so I knew he was up there. He knew I had come because the door opened as I walked down the hushed corridor. It shut with a heavy click behind me.

He was undressed, wrapped in a large, white, deep-pile courtesy towel. A damp film of moisture put a shine on his sand-coloured skin and snaked through his darkened hair. The smell of sandalwood drifted over me.

'Would you like a shower?' he said.

I felt dirty all right, and it wasn't just the heat, the ride through the fume-hazy streets, and the bar smell that clung to my breath and my blouse. A shower would have been wonderful but I wanted a fight first.

17

'I don't want a bloody shower. I want to know why you did that.'

'I don't understand.'

'Back there? Why did you do that?'

'What?'

'You hurt me.'

'Oh, that.'

He walked into the bathroom and I heard the shower start like welcome rain.

'Did you find my presentation interesting?' he said, coming back to the doorway.

'What?'

'At the conference.'

'I missed it.'

'Pity.'

'I had to get dressed, remember?'

I swayed defiantly by the double bed. No twins for us, but I wasn't fooled by the promise of intimacy. It was a purely practical consideration. My reflection in the three high mirrors above the rich mahogany headboard was shabby and peevish, whichever way I looked at it. My hair needed brushing. My face was greasy with perspiration.

'Better take off your clothes,' he said, handing me a large towel like his own.

'I'm not staying.'

He shrugged. I kicked off my shoes and swung my handbag into the chair.

'You bastard.'

I might as well have thrown a dandelion clock through the air. Glancing first at his watch, he turned his back and I heard the shower cut out. Then he walked past me into the room's open-plan lounge and switched the television on. A familiar face with authoritative boxed shoulders appeared onscreen. It was the late afternoon news round-up. He stood watching it, arms folded, still, with his pale freckled back to me. I wanted to rake at it but the cursed urge to kiss it instead tugged like a hangnail.

'Please, David. Talk to me.'

What a pathetic little whine. I hated myself. Mentally, I was on my knees. The big deal newsreader wound up with a slick, patronizing smile and handed over to the local man. Then we had the weather and a gratuitously violent cartoon for kids followed. David turned down the sound, and turned to the low, glass coffee table. He plucked a white tissue from its slim box and with soft, gentle, circular movements wiped some condensation from the lenses of his spectacles. His myopic eyes seemed larger and bluer as he looked up to settle the metallic frames back on to his face. He spoke with surprisingly little irritation. 'I do what I do because you want me to.'

It took me a while to think what to say. What came out didn't amount to a whole lot.

'Oh yes?' I said, lifting my chin to challenge him.

'I'm quite happy to oblige,' he said, screwing up the tissue into a tight ball. He held it high in the fist of his hand before dropping it into the peach velveteen-covered bin. He smiled to himself, satisfied no doubt in another safe little confirmation of the theory of gravity.

I sat down heavily on the bed. It took a moment or two for my voice to settle at the pitch at which I wanted it. I should have taken a little longer. 'You are unbelievable,' I shrieked.

There was no reaction. He wasn't really paying attention. He was watching the television again, not listening to me. I wanted to make him listen so I yelled a little louder.

'You . . . arrogant . . . arrogant . . . little shit. You started all this. In bloody New York. You ring me up every time you're in town. Do I ever call you? Well? Do I? Who's obliging who? Uh?'

He didn't even turn his head. He watched the frenetic activity on the box come to a crushing end before walking over to the sofa beyond by the table and sitting down, elbows on his knees. There was a box of matches on the table. He stretched out a hand, picked it up, opened it and began. One by one, he picked them up and broke each match in half or bent them into arrows. I watched for as long as I could bear before walking gingerly over the soft carpet to where he sat. I stood between him and the soundless television. My lowered voice was woolly from the drink.

'What is it you like?' I said.

He snapped a few more matches and then looked up at me, his eyes clear, direct and untroubled. 'You want me to tell you?'

'Yes.'

'Are you sure it wouldn't spoil things?'

No, dear, things are just dandy. I stared down at him, wishing there was a match left to set fire to his little pile of splinters. 'No,' I said.

'I like working you over. I like that.'

The sentence carried all the sensuality of a contract of employment. I worked for him. He worked me over.

'Very nice. And do you know what I like, exactly?'

'I know what you like. I prove it every time.'

'So what is it?'

'Does it matter?'

'It does. Because I don't think I do like it.'

'Then why are you here?'

'Not all of it, anyway.'

Snap. Snap. Snap. The pile of sticks grew.

'Death,' he said.

'What?'

'You heard.'

'But I don't want to die,' I said.

'I know that.'

20

'I don't understand.'

'You like to feel it coming.'

'I do?'

'Believe me. That's what you like.'

With a neat flick, he threw the empty matchbox in an arc, so perfectly considered that it landed with a dull clatter in the bin. The air in the room felt heavy and thick, like the accumulated breath of animals in a cave. I turned quickly, half falling over the furniture in my efforts to gather up my shoes and handbag.

'Excuse me,' I said, making for the door, but he was there already. He grasped my chin firmly in one hand, while the other grasped the soft meat between my thighs.

'Reusable. Like a glass. I can make death reusable for you. Fill it up. Empty it. Start all over again. See?'

Tears started from my eyes and I blinked. Everything inside me seemed to collapse. I didn't know why I didn't fight, push him aside and leave. I hung there like a rabbit pulled from a hat until he let me go.

'You go ahead and have a shower. Have a rest. Have a drink. There's lots in the cabinet,' he said. 'I've got work to do.'

As I lay naked on the bed watching the early evening television, a couple of miniatures ready on the bedside table, David read some papers. My mind pottered through an endless loop of thoughts to no resolution. Death. He thought he'd seen it in my mind and wanted it out here in the real world, so our fantasies could mix and match. I wanted it back in my head so that I could switch the action off. I didn't want it in the real world. It was too real in the real world. It was too thrilling for a rapt child to be read a tale of cruel wolves, by the cruellest wolf of all. Be careful what you wish for, as mama said. Call the whole thing off. That would be the best thing. Just call the whole grotesque thing off.

CHAPTER THREE

Julie Wentworth said she'd be in the back bar and that she'd be wearing a blue denim jacket and a black straw hat. The hat was pulled down to her mousy eyebrows and, with the wall lights behind her, its large, upturned, crescent-shaped brim looked like an eclipse of the moon. She was reading the evening paper.

'Julie Wentworth?'

She turned to me. Her tanned face was bare of make-up but for a smear of translucent gloss on her fleshy lips and a curl of mascara on her short, sparse lashes. She had good bones, full cheekbones, a strong jaw line and small, dark brown eyes, deep-set and rather close together. She had a hard, bright, intelligent look about her, and she certainly took a long look at me before folding her paper and placing it neatly by her glass. 'Georgina Powers?'

'Yes.'

She raised her small, elegant hand and placed it firmly in mine, grasping it with the other. 'So pleased to meet you.'

I tried to pull my hand back but she wasn't ready. She held it firmly until I had taken a seat beside her.

'I can't tell you how grateful I am to you for sparing your time.'

The soft roll of her 'r's exposed a Scots accent under the southern. I shifted my sunglasses up my nose so they sat snug and tight around my eyes.

'Well, if it's a story, I could be grateful to you,' I said and tapped the dark lenses in front of my eyes. 'Excuse the glasses, light sensitivity.'

She pushed a small glass of house white towards me and put her own glass to her lips. I pulled a fresh packet of twenty from my bag. I offered, she shook her head and I lit up. She stared at me as I went through my routine. I didn't ask if she minded.

'Well,' I said, exhaling a plume of fresh smoke up above our heads, 'what have you got?'

She took a 3.5-inch disk from her bag. 'I've got this.'

'What about it?'

'It's pornography. Like the stuff you were writing about. The filth that those kids were downloading from the public computerized bulletin boards.'

I wasn't that interested unless she could tell me the source. The story was done. There was a lot of it about. 'Did you get it from one of the boards?' I said.

She pointed at herself, her eyes wide with mock innocence. '*Moi?*'

'Who then?' I said.

'It's my husband's. It's his bloody problem, not mine.'

'How'd you get it?'

'I found it while . . .'

'. . . Looking through his things?'

I got a sharp look from those beady dormouse eyes, and flicked some ash into the ashtray. Time to get to the point. 'He makes it?'

'I'm not sure.'

'Well, is he a VIP or what?'

She looked confused but I didn't want to waste any time. 'Look I don't know what sort of relationship you have, and to be honest, Julie, I don't care. It isn't that big a deal for an ordinary guy to get off on porn, not as far as the papers I work for are concerned. It is, of course, if

23

he's the source of the stuff or if he's a Very Important Person.'

'I see.'

'Is he?'

No reply.

'Look, don't be disappointed. Last week, we had computer kids getting their hands on mainstream stuff by dialling a number. This week, we have to move on.'

She nodded and pushed the disk across the wooden table top towards me. 'Perhaps you ought to run it and see for yourself,' she said.

She was looking at me right in the face again, undeterred by the dark glasses shielding my eyes. I didn't know what she was looking for. If she wanted me to share her outrage, she was going to be disappointed. I wasn't the right person for outrage and anyway, I didn't believe she'd chased me to ground just for me to throw up my hands. There had to be something else that I could do for her.

We finished our drinks and I took her down the side streets to Old Compton Street and the office. Unless she was a plastic card junkie, we were quite safe. Soho's neon-lit sleaze was losing its battle against the restrained glow of designer uplighting in the smart little retail outlets and decently bohemian food emporia that lined the way. Just a thin straggle of strip-joints flashed like strands of a whirling, threadbare tassel among the chic new frontages.

The offices of *Technology Week* maintained a haughty air of shabbiness. It was 7.30 p.m. and there were still some people working upstairs. A muffled voice let us in. Max was behind his desk, of course, on the phone to somewhere, tuning into the ether for some transatlantic information wire. He didn't bother to look up as we pushed through the double doors into the vast fluores-cent-lit space, littered by paper and grubby machines.

24

Richard's homely desk seemed as good as anywhere so I walked over and sat down. Julie didn't; she looked around and whispered.

'I don't want anyone else to see this. Isn't there another office?'

'Nope. This is it. Don't worry. No one's going to come over. Stand behind me if you like,' I said.

She didn't look happy but I powered up Richard's machine and stuck in my password all the same. I still had some space on the company network. She stood close to my shoulder, nervous as a downwind deer. I felt her stiffen up when I opened the file. The graphics came up for just over thirty seconds in black and white. It was a shock, I admit, even though I had got used to watching the stuff. Some of it made me laugh. I mean, even I can see the funny side of Pacman gobbling around a screen with a hard-on. Unfortunately, most computer pornography is as dull as the real thing.

They say that there are just five jokes in the world and all the rest are variations. Well, the plots in mainstream porn, whatever the medium, are no more original. You know, the lonely housewife, the casting couch, the party, doctors and nurses, and boy meets girl. You get a few stock heterosexual scenarios with a few three-way and lesbian scenes thrown in like bay leaves in a thin stock. Rape is not a common theme and the bizarre stuff is strictly a niche market. The fact is that mainstream sex scenes are more formulaic than Mills and Boon. Apart from graphics stuff, most computer porn is converted from porn movies anyway. So far so boring, until now. Until now, I'd never seen anyone I knew in one.

Up on the screen were just a few grainy frames of what is described, in the trade, as a blow job, and not a very competent one, in my humble opinion. The fact that I recognized the woman was what made it really special. The man, I couldn't pick out of a line-up, but it was

25

definitely her. It was definitely Julie Wentworth. I hit the button and the screen directory displayed its sparse, discreet menu. She was crouching beside me now, looking up at me with defiant earnestness.

'Julie . . . um, this really is between you and your . . .'

'I didn't do it,' she said.

'Look, I can see that it's you, and I don't even know you that well.'

'I'm telling you, I didn't do it. Do I look like the sort of girl that does that?'

I didn't answer. Well, what kind of a question is that?

'Well, do I?' she said.

'Look, all sorts of quite nice girls . . .'

'I didn't do it.'

Her bright little night eyes were supercharged with indignation. She must have looked at that black and white lollipop sequence a thousand times and it still stoked her up. I leaned back to Diane's desk and pulled over a chair so she could sit down. She sat on the edge, fiddling with the handle of her handbag.

'It's me. Of course it is. But it's a fake. Take it from me, I've never done that,' she said.

I didn't like to run the thing again, but I felt I had to. This time I took a more dispassionate look. It did look wrong. Her eyes were open for a start and it looked as if, well, it looked as if she was chewing the thing off.

'It's possible, I suppose,' I said, switching the program off again. 'How much do you know about computers?'

'A bit. My husband's the expert. I pick things up.'

Now if I had been a dog, my ears would have pointed forward along with my cold, damp, twitching nose. If he was a heap big expert, there was the angle. Maybe he was just a smutty little programmer fabricating his own porn from innocent, or not so innocent, videos. A computer porn manufacturer, a digital porn factory. There was a great angle in that, too. And what if there were more like him or more copies of the program in circulation?

'I've got an idea how it could be done. You can tell me, if it fits in with anything,' I said.

'OK.' She sounded bitter but determined.

I took the disk out and handed it back to her. She pushed it back to me.

'OK. Have you got a video or video stills camera at home?' I said.

She nodded and I popped a cigarette into my mouth. She watched my lips wrap around and draw in until I felt as self-conscious as if it had been me on the screen. I wasn't about to deny anything. Any politician will tell you that's the worst thing you can be made to do. I pulled the cigarette from my mouth. 'Which?'

'Both.'

'Right. If your husband's into computers, he might have a frame grabber,' I said.

'I don't know what that is.'

'OK. It's possible to digitize photographic images and display them on a computer screen. For still photographs, you need a scanner, but for moving video images, you need a video digitizer – a frame grabber.'

The full implication of what I was explaining only began to dawn when I told her the rest. That, once digitized, those images could be stored, and with the right software, manipulated.

'What do you mean, manipulated?' she said.

'Changed. Tidied up. Smooth out rough edges. Alter them. Put things in that weren't there before, remove things that were. It's not difficult or expensive. You can do it on an ordinary PC. One of these.'

'I see.'

'Stalin would have loved it.'

'I bet.'

'Any ideas?' I said.

27

'Well, we've got home videos, of course.'

I raised an eyebrow.

'Nothing unusual in that.' She had a right to sound defensive. She knew what I was going to ask. She probably had the offending video in mind. I was trying to be professional about it but really I was busting to laugh.

'Any that could be teased around to make you look as if . . .?' I said.

'Oh, give me a break. You mean, have I got any close-ups of me eating a banana or something?'

'You said it.'

'D'you really think I'd find it now?'

She sat in silence while I smoked my cigarette. I took my time over it, just to let her calm down. She was a good sulker. Her lips turned down and her eyebrows flexed into a rumple of flesh above her nose. After a while in this pose, she sighed and said: 'From what I understood from your article this would be easy to distribute to a wider audience.'

I shrugged. Of course. She knew that. I took my chance then. 'Look, it's probably for his own pleasure. Perhaps you could talk about it. I mean a man with a respectable, well-paid job isn't about to start selling mail order, is he? Talk to him.'

That lit the fuse. The brim of her chic black hat bobbed forward aggressively. Her strong chin came at me too.

'Talk to him? He's the proverbial brick wall. Talk about his job, his computers, his work. Fine. Talk about anything else to Dr David Jones, forget it.'

She may have been leading with her chin but I got it fair and square on mine. She might as well have hit me with a ball hammer and the impact sent my mind gabbling backwards to when she'd said his name. Dr David Jones. How many were there, for God's sake? Computer expert. Dr David Jones. It had to be him. My eyes burned behind my glasses.

'Dr David Jones, the virtual reality guy?'

'The very same.'

'But you're . . .'

'I like to use my maiden name.'

I garnered my shattered self-control. I wanted to ease her away. Away out of the double door, back down the bright Soho streets to wherever she had come from. But I was cool about it, switching off the machine and handing her back her disk.

'I'm sorry, it's still not a story I'm interested in – unless you want to expose yourself, and your husband, to the full horror of the tabloids,' I said.

'I don't understand.'

'They'd kill for it but, to be honest, it's not my kind of story. Take my advice. Go home. Work this one out between yourselves.'

'Look, I don't want you to print anything,' she said.

'Then why come to me?'

'I wanted your help. I saw your story in the papers. I thought you'd know how a program like this was put together.'

'Now you know.'

'Now I know.'

'Dangerous game.'

'I had to take a chance on you.'

'So, go home.'

'Look, what if my husband didn't fake them? What if someone else did and sent it to him, to blackmail him? He does have a very important job, you know . . . Now, that's a story, isn't it?'

I knew how important his job was. I knew a lot of other things, too. It struck me that if she was shocked by the prospect of a blow job, she had no concept of what her husband really liked to do. My thoughts scrambled towards damage limitation, but she was still talking, getting desperate.

'Someone might be blackmailing him, don't you see?' she said.

I didn't answer, I was looking around for my bag. I wanted to leave but she grabbed my hand.

'Look, I thought that, as a woman, you could help me,' she said.

I wanted to shrink to nothing, to a tiny mote of innocence. She wanted to share her problem with me because we were sisters under the skin. What we really were were sisters under his skin. We were rivals for his kiss. I had won a deadly mark of faithlessness and she the tender expression of marital love. I had never been with a married man before David. I'd never been confronted by the wife of a lover or even the lover of a lover. I steered away from other people's mates. I'd caught my own husband with my best friend and it had ended in divorce. I'd blundered into the privacy of my own home and pulled open the curtains on someone else's, to the sight and sound of them spreading apart before my eyes. It wasn't something I wanted to inflict on someone else.

I began to feel warm and edgy in my loose T-shirt. I looked at Julie Wentworth's desperate face. What was she really doing here? I reached for and lit another cigarette before noticing the last one burning in the ashtray.

'If you think that someone's trying to blackmail your husband, call the police,' I said.

I tried to get up but she grabbed me again. 'I've got another one.'

'Where?'

'At home.'

'The same?'

'No.'

'Why didn't you bring it?'

'I was scared.'

Scared wasn't the same as embarrassed.

'Why?'

Glassy tears spilled on to her cheeks. She started to blub. Her nose began to drip and she brushed the back of one pretty hand against it. I couldn't feel sorry for her. I hated her for exposing me.

'I hid it,' she said.

'Why?'

'He's on it.'

I tensed up and then relaxed. No, it couldn't be me. 'Oh?' I said, stubbing out the burning cigarette.

'And it's worse.'

I waited.

'I think he's killed someone.'

CHAPTER FOUR

David and I had met for lunch. I had wanted to sit out on the pavement in the sunshine but he took a table inside.

'You'll burn,' he said to me. 'In this heat.'

I took a breadstick and skewered it into the butter. 'I never burn,' I said.

'I find that hard to believe.'

'I go brown.'

'But you never are.'

'No.'

I crunched the stick and pointed the crooked end at his arms. 'You've got a nice colour,' I said.

'I play tennis.'

'How nice.'

I looked away because he was staring at me and not speaking. I didn't want to look into his eyes. I tried to look indifferent, crunching the breadstick and looking around.

'Is something wrong?' he said.

'Oh no.'

He pulled at one soft downy earlobe and then lifted his hand to call the waiter. I had to tell him. 'You're married, aren't you?' I said.

He turned back to look at me, his spectacles glinting in the light. When the waiter arrived, he ordered quickly and sent him away. 'Yes.'

'I guessed.'

'How?'

'If you aren't married, why do we meet like this?'

It was obvious but I hadn't thought about it before. I thought the hotel rooms were part of the game. Of course they were.

'Does it matter?' he said, raising his glass of Campari.

'Of course it does,' I said, putting down mine.

'Why?'

'You're married, for God's sake.'

'Do you want to marry me?'

'No.'

'Well then. It doesn't matter.' He clinked his bitter fruitdrop drink against my glass. 'Drink up.'

'Why? Do you like me drunk?'

'A little.'

'A lot.'

'All right. A lot.'

The waiter came with our lunch. I waited until he'd gone before I whispered across the table. 'It does matter. I feel guilty about her.'

'Don't. I don't.'

'Well, I do.'

'She doesn't know.'

'How do you know she doesn't know?'

'She'd kill me if she found out, that's why.'

'I suppose you think that's funny.'

'No. Why?'

'Never mind. Have you had other affairs?'

'Yes.'

'Did she find out?'

'Yes.'

'And?'

'Nothing.'

He waited, but I didn't ask why not. I looked away from him around the warm, light-coloured restaurant

33

with its bright murals of green and brown fruit-laden islands set in azure seas.

'The blue veins on the inside of your arms . . .' he said.

'Don't.'

'The skin there is so soft and white.'

'Don't.'

The waiter hovered again by the table. David ordered more wine. My heart was beating so hard I was afraid everyone might hear it. I didn't know how far I could go. I was afraid, but I wanted to see what he would do. I wanted him to astonish me.

'I've got a room,' he said.

'No.'

He looked up from slicing the pale meat on his plate. 'Are you saying it's over?'

'I want you to explain.'

'You want me to talk about her.'

'No.'

'What then?'

'Why would this affair bother her more?'

I'd asked but he wouldn't answer. I looked down at the woven pasta and placed my knife and fork neatly on either side of my plate. I lifted my glass and drained it dry. More wine came and I drank that too until the lunchtime crowd began to thin out. It was still hot outside but the table where I'd wanted to sit was in shade. Two people were sitting there laughing together. He was nice, she was nice. Everyone was nice, so nice that I wanted to cry. David placed his tiny, empty espresso cup in its thick china saucer.

'I know what you like,' he said softly.

'What you like, you mean.'

'I know what you like.'

'I don't like you.'

He slid the address of the chosen hotel across the table to me. I took it but didn't unfold the paper.

'I won't come,' I said, looking down at it. I felt as if my legs were caught by an undertow. It was too hard to play with him. It had to be real, but if it was real I'd go under. I looked up to catch his eye. He looked young for thirty-eight, smooth-faced and fair. His eyes were like the sky, blue, and, yes, all over me. Oh boy, there was that look. In anyone else it would have meant hearts and flowers, wine and dine, long kisses, diamonds and gold, and then, come live with me and be my love. With him it was darkness and dread, vertiginous walls and airless corners, matchwood, driftwood, weeds and wolf moons.

'Your bones are so beautiful I could break them,' he said.

'Why don't you have this instead,' I replied, handing him a broken, buttered wand of bread.

Of course, I turned up. The room in Victoria wasn't like the others. It was in one of those large, sad houses in a square where you'd imagine a carriage drawing up with a well-dressed family of mama, papa and delightfully dressed children aboard. The house, with its creamy pillars and marbled steps, had lately been pressed into service. The porter in the dim lobby gave me a key with a number and I made my way up the stairs to a narrow, musty corridor and a hastily painted plasterboard door. Behind it was a single room with its long, yellowish curtains drawn and most of the space taken up by a narrow lumpy bed, square white sink and brown veneered wardrobe. I wiped my clammy palms on my dress. I had no plan, no reason to come, just compulsion. I looked around the walls, expecting spiders, but there were none. I started at a knocking, like a wooden brush against a skirting board. It was cool in the room, and quiet but for cars whirring in the street below. I stood as still as a mouse in a cold cave of air, waiting for an earth in the static. I could hear my blood drumming hotly past my ears. Time to leave, run, run, run. I turned but the door clicked shut. He didn't say anything.

'You made me jump,' I said.

'How high?'

'I don't want to stay. Let me out.'

'Scream,' he said.

I just stared at him.

'Scream. Someone will come running. There's a traveller on either side, a whore across the way, the porter downstairs. They'll come.'

'I'm not going to scream. Let me pass,' I said.

He didn't, of course; he walked me backwards until my back pressed against the side of the wardrobe. It was cold and slightly damp against the scoop of skin between my shoulder blades. He dragged his hands over my shoulders and pressed my covered breasts.

'Are you drunk?' he said.

'No more than usual,' I replied.

'Are you afraid?'

'What do you think?'

'Then we can find out about each other,' he said and took his glasses off.

There were no tricks this time. My dread retreated into passion. His hands were tender with my flesh and his mouth soft and strong on mine. I wanted him, believed in him and when it was over, I fell asleep in his arms. Deep asleep from afternoon light until summer darkness, until the rhythmic movement of his body against mine woke me. With my eyes half open, I looked across the pillow and saw his metal-framed glasses folded by an empty tumbler beside the bed. I wasn't sure at first that I was awake. My senses were sluggish, weighted by the lunchtime Camparis and wine. The room was in darkness but for the gloomy half-light of a lamp in the street. He felt me stirring but didn't stop; instead, he moved more languidly as if not to wake me. I chose to close my eyes again and let him rock but the half-glimpse of his chalk-whitened hand, gripping my chalk-whitened wrist, startled me. I lay watching it until, with eyes opened wide, I looked straight up at his face.

He was staring right back, his eyes stark in a dusty mask. I looked down over my dusted body. It was paler than moonlight, a strong, sickly perfume rising from it to catch my breath. My mouth was dry as glass paper, my lips moist and sticky. I could taste plums and bitter almonds. His hands loosened their grip, smoothed softly up to my shoulders, then touched my neck. He stroked my skin gently with pallid fingers that stretched around and under my hair, spreading it out over the pillow before they came back to hold my throat, gently at first like a child holding a bird, but then too tightly, far too tightly to breathe.

'David?'

'Ssh.'

'David?'

He slowly began to squeeze the breath from me until my instincts kicked in and I pushed violently upwards. He loosened his grip a little.

'Close your eyes. Keep still,' he said. His darkened lips glistened in the half-light and I found my half-strangled voice.

'For Christ's sake. What are you doing?'

'Don't talk. Keep still.'

'Get off me. Please. Please.'

'Ssh. It's all right.'

'Don't, David. You're choking me.'

'Don't talk. It's all right.'

It didn't feel all right. It didn't feel all right at all. Panic made me struggle but as I jerked up again, his hands pressed harder. He squeezed slowly and relentlessly until I couldn't take in the slightest whistle of air. My eyes

37

seemed to bulge outwards like a bullfrog's neck, stretching like a bubble-gum ball. A terrible pain surged through my head and I could hear myself grunting, feel myself passing out. Then the pressure eased off and the air wheezed down my throat. I gulped and gulped like a drowning swimmer breaking surface. But he squeezed again and I could do nothing but stare up at his crazy, ecstatic face and pray to a God I'd forgotten long ago. I prayed, but the person who came to mind was my mother, sitting on a red tartan blanket pouring tea from a flask. I could hear it and her calling to me as the midday sun beat down upon my head. The tide was going out and the pressure in my skull pumped up and up. The pain grew again like a tumour. He squeezed and released, squeezed and released, on and on, until I lay limp and he shook soundlessly, like a man drenched in melting ice. I'll never forget his face. It was the wan, untroubled face of a man at peace; the face of a dead man.

'We have an understanding, don't we?' he said.

I nodded meekly.

'You understand what I want. I understand what you want.'

I said nothing.

'Answer me.'

'Yes.'

'It's wonderful, isn't it?'

'Yes.'

His dry temperate hands stroked my body and the white dust moved around in swirls.

'What is it?' I asked, my voice thick with fear and pain. He licked his finger and drew a wet circle broken by an arrow on the ivory curve of my hip.

'Oriental face powder. Like chalk, only finer, and perfumed. See, you're as smooth as a bone.'

His mouth was close, his face was as pale as bleached linen.

'Why me?' I said.

'You let me.'

'You said there were others.'

'Yes.'

'So?'

'It's the look. You never wear colours, do you?'

'No?'

'Just black or white.'

'Oh.'

'And underneath, you're the same. White skin. Dark hair. Bruised eyes, lips.'

'It's a hard life being a fashion victim,' I said, turning quickly to move off the bed, but he was quicker. He pulled me back towards him, stained lips stretching over his creamy teeth in a rare, magnetic smile. I put a finger to my face to wipe away a tear and the pale powder came away on to my hand. He leaned over my shoulder and kissed me. I could taste the sweet lipstick and feel the meaty roll of his tongue. He kissed me softly, at first, and then hard, very, very hard.

'My God, Georgina.'

'Hi.'

'What the hell's happened?'

'Nothing.'

'You look like a zombie.'

'Thanks.'

'Are you all right?'

'Uh huh.'

I was looking for a drink by the dim light from the hallway when I tripped over Richard. He'd fallen asleep on the sofa wearing his headphones and now he'd switched the room light full on so that I stood blinking uncomfortably in its glare like a bush baby surprised by a cameraman's flash. He peered at my face.

'Have you been crying?' he said.

'No.'

'Your hair's wet. Your neck. Streuth, your eyes.'

'My eyes?'

'What's happened?'

It was 2 a.m. and I didn't want to talk about it. Every nerve in my body seemed to be nibbling at my skin. I felt sick, my throat was raw and my head felt as if something with a tough beak was trying very hard to get out. I decided against the gin. I needed water. Richard followed me into the kitchen.

'Georgina . . .'

'Leave it, Richard. Please.'

He waited while I filled a glass and guzzled it down. I retched, refilled the glass and tried again. It was hard to swallow so I took my time this time, resting every now and then, my head hanging over the sink.

'Georgina . . .'

'For Christ's sake . . . just leave it.'

'All right. All right.'

I didn't move from the sink and he wouldn't move from behind me. He waited and then spoke gently. 'Your mother phoned three times. They want to see you.'

'Great. My mother. Got any paracetamol? Morphine?'

He dug two pills from his medicine box and passed them to me. I swallowed them with difficulty, rinsed the glass and put it on the drainer. Time was when I'd have just left it in the sink with all the rest of the junk, but Richard, though a little sloppy elsewhere, liked a clean, organized kitchen. He liked to cook. His flat, his rules.

'I saw them at Christmas,' I said.

'George. It's August.'

'So?'

He rolled his eyes. 'I've given you the message, all right?'

'All right.'

'Can I do anything for you?'

'No . . . thanks.'

He turned and went muttering to his room. I took the glass, filled it up again and went to mine. I lay there with the side light on. I'd tried the darkness but I didn't like it. With the light on I could see that this was my room, cluttered with my debris and my PC on my desk in the corner. I wondered if the window was shut. I hoped it was because I was afraid to get up and see.

Richard's face peered at me over the duvet. I turned away from him, pushing my head into the pillow where the bright sun was drawing a thick line through a break in the curtains.

'George. George. Wake up. Georgina.'

I covered my face.

'George, wake up. You must wake up. Come on, love. It's Sunday morning.'

Sunday morning. What happened to Saturday? I sat up quickly, remembering to hang on to the bedcovers as I did so.

'How long have I slept?' I said.

Richard didn't reply. His face was all awrinkle with concern.

My voice broke as I spoke again. 'What are you staring at?'

'Your face.'

'That good, eh?'

'I never liked the Mekon myself.'

Wrapping the thick duvet around myself, I inched off the bed, hobbled over to my dressing table and sat down in a bundle on a chair in front of it. The mirror justified Richard's concern. I appeared to be wearing a necklet of purple and yellow bruises and my eyeballs were beaded with broken blood vessels. The inside of my swollen lips felt sore where my teeth had cut in and I still found it hard to swallow. I leaned dizzily forward to the mirror for a close-up.

'You know what?' I said.

'What?'

'I think I've got flu.'

'Yeah, and Mrs T's just a shy girl from Grantham.'

I looked in my bag for my brush. There was the note with the hotel and room number on, and there was the one with Diane's large script and the name, Julie Wentworth. I tried to remember what she'd rung for, what Richard had said.

'Come on, I'm taking you up to the hospital,' he said.

'What for?' I said, brushing my hair briskly.

'For an oil change. What do you think? For a medical check-up, for God's sake.'

'So I'm a Mekon with flu, so what?'

'Don't be flip. You look terrible.'

'Look, Richard, this didn't happen in an alley.'

'Someone you knew did this?'

'Yes.'

'Come on. I'm taking you up there.'

I slammed the brush on the table and spilled the tea he had brought me. 'Don't. Leave it. I know where I've been hurt. Leave it,' I said.

'The police then.'

'No.'

'Why not?'

'Forget it.'

'You can't let him get away with this.'

I didn't answer.

'Look, if he can do this to you . . . well, he could do it to someone else.'

'I wish he would, Richard. I really wish he would.'

Richard turned and left the room with an angry pull on the door. He'd wanted me to confess, if only for the sake of crime prevention. Poor Richard. He didn't understand. The police wouldn't, either. How could I explain? We've got this thing, see. He's the Angel of Death and I'm Everywoman. He scares me until I feel as horny as hell. You can understand that, can't you? I'll bet. No, I didn't want a doctor's gloved hands, a policeman's hard eyes, or their questions, probing me. I wasn't a victim, after all. I was an accomplice.

I sat looking at my image in the mirror, a hastily daubed and dabbed travesty of myself. Beneath the thumbmark bruises and sorry aches, little ideas were starting to stir like bubbles in champagne in a dark bottle. All was not lost. There was a story in it if I could follow through. I amazed myself. Was it conditioning or genes? There was the headline. The life and loves of a top computer expert. My night of hell with Doctor Death. Would you trust this man with a military computer? No, it was no good, I couldn't do it.

I wasn't that kind of journalist, was I?

CHAPTER FIVE

The telephone rang in the hall and I heard a soft knocking at my door.

'Come in,' I said. It was Richard.

'Some chap on the phone. Won't give his name. Says you know him.'

'OK, thanks.'

Richard padded back down the hall to his kitchen which was marinating in the sweet aromas of our evening meal, warmed by puffs of steam, sunlight and the vibrant sound of Vivaldi. My cool room was in shadow now. It caught the morning sun, which bounced off the flat greasy surface of the Grand Union for a few hours before hoisting itself over the chimney pots. Then it shone down on the front of the house, its narrow steps and the old road that separated us from the vast green spread of Victoria Park. Richard had bought the large three-bedroomed house before the rampant property boom and had patched it and pampered it until it had regained its former poise. It was worth a bit now, and I helped ease the slight burden of his mortgage with rent. Not that I didn't have money. I had a lot of it, lying untouched in a bank, increasing with interest like a dark, discarded blob of jam crusting with mould. It had come to me as an unwanted gift from a former friend and I liked to pretend that I hadn't got it. Stubborn pride, if you like, but it wasn't my ill-gotten money.

Richard had an idea who was calling me and his disapproval hung in the room. He had never mentioned that night again, but his sense of honour and justice had been badly bruised. Now David was intruding into his own home like frost in a greenhouse. I had his wife's disk in my room, the merest snapshot of a dysfunctioning sexuality. My heart was drumming in my chest, beating out that rhythm of fear that I welcomed and wanted whenever he was near.

'Hello.'

''Ello, it's me.'

Wrong. All wrong. Hello, this is David, maybe. Medium-paced, accentless, matter-of-fact. That's what I was expecting. I was not expecting what I heard.

'I'm sorry. Who is this?'

He replied but I could barely hear, what with the clatter of dishes and the Vivaldi. Maybe I did hear, but couldn't believe it.

'Hold on,' I said, and went to close the kitchen door. 'Hello?'

There was nothing but the rapid pipping sound of a lost coin-box call. I replaced the receiver and walked slowly into the kitchen.

'Richard?'

He was ladling red sauce over some handsome fish. 'Ready?' he said, looking up.

'What did that guy sound like to you?'

'Some East End oik.'

He didn't mean that really. He was getting at me for letting David get away with murder. I sat down at the kitchen table.

'Mind your elbows. The plate's hot,' he said, ill-temperedly waving his hand at me. I sat back, hands folded on my lap, as he squeezed some lemon over slices of lightly oiled courgettes.

When at last he sat down he said: 'Where is the wine?'

enunciating every word simply and purposefully for the benefit of the simpleton opposite. She was gazing out somewhere into the middle distance.

'Oi!'

I jumped.

'The wine.'

I got up from my chair, apologizing, and brought over the bottle of Californian red, pouring a generous amount into Richard's large glass goblet.

'What about you?' he said, having watched me sit down with an unusually empty glass. I didn't respond, so he leaned over with a sigh and poured me a rich raspberry-thick glassful.

'Why don't you kick this guy into touch? You've hardly been out of this place in weeks. You've done no work. Get rid of him.'

'It wasn't him. It was someone else,' I said, slicing the fish off the bone. Richard grunted and placed a well-laden fork into his mouth.

I knew a few people who spoke like that but only two of them men who'd call me at home, and only one of them knew where I lived. He bristled with portable telephones and would have said who he was. No reason not to. The other had disappeared after making himself rich at everyone else's expense. Warren Graham. It couldn't be Warren Graham. It had to be a wrong number. No, he'd asked for me and he hadn't given his name. Maybe he thought I wouldn't have come to the phone. Bloody right. How did he get my number?

'Hello?' Richard was calling to me from across the table.

I looked up. 'Huh?'

'Oh, I bloody well give up,' he said, dumping his napkin on the cluttered table.

'I'm sorry.'

'I'm sick of it.'

'I'm sorry.'

'Look, it's a beautiful evening. How about a walk? You know, outside, open the door, down the steps, clippety-clop.'

'I don't want a walk.'

'Let's go for a walk.'

'No.'

'OK. How about an amble to the pub for a jar or two? Diane'll be there. Oh. Oh, my God. What's that on your face?'

It was a smile, for the girl who had made it.

'Diane?' I said.

'She mentioned that she liked jazz.'

'Did she mention that she liked you too?'

He started collecting up the dishes. 'You wash, I'll dry,' he said.

'Mmm, great. Don't we have fun.'

I couldn't understand why we always had to do this little chore straight away, but Richard had insisted too many times for me to argue. Warren would love to see this: me up to my elbows in yellow Marigold gloves and kind-to-your-hands soap bubbles. I was certain it was him. How could I forget his voice? The nasty devious turncoat. I thought of the money in the bank. He could have it back now, and the mouldy interest. I'd gladly watch him eat it.

Richard put the final piece of cutlery in its correct compartment in the drawer and pointed at the table for me to wipe. He looked down at himself. His sweatshirt had a couple of bright food stains down the front, but the jeans and trainers looked OK.

'I think I'd better change. What about you?' he said.

'Look, you go. There's something I want to see on the TV tonight,' I said.

He looked at me as if I'd insulted his mother. 'Do you know what it has been like living with you lately?'

'Bad, eh?'

'Bad? I'll tell you bad. I can handle the slob in you, George. I can handle the drunk. I can even handle the smartass. What I cannot handle is the dull, depressed, vacant-eyed agoraphobic house mouse.'

'Hey, who are you calling a drunk?'

'Shut up. It's been like living in a bloody morgue with a corpse that makes the tea occasionally.'

'I'm sorry.'

'He's got to you and you won't do a bloody thing about it.'

'Richard . . .'

He pointed a finger at me and large muscles clenched along his reddish tanned arm. 'No bloody excuses, Georgina. You're coming out for some fresh air and a few laughs. Right? Now get dressed.'

I'd never really seen Richard take full command. We shared a house, after all; there had to be some give and take. Now for a moment I could see what Diane saw. He looked quite good. All the slack was pulled up and he'd grown a couple of inches taller. If I was a bloke, I wouldn't mess with him. My hands came up in surrender.

'I'll come but I won't stay. All right?'

'Don't you like Diane?'

'Very much. But I've got a purple neck and red eyes. I don't need to be green and hairy as well.'

He stared at me, hands on hips, gut pushed out as I walked past him out of the door. It took me ten minutes to get ready and Richard, twenty. He showered, combed back what was left of his curly light brown hair and put on a fresh cotton shirt with clean chinos. He smelled like a spice merchant in a lemon grove. I stood by him fingering the high roll neck of a black Lycra halter top.

'Am I covered?' I said.

'Yes, but in a thing that tight it's a matter of opinion.'

I hit his proffered elbow before starting through the

open door. Once on the outside step, I stopped and turned back. Richard barred my way with a tough look. 'Glasses,' I said and pushed past him.

They were on the table in the lounge, by the window. I picked them up and glanced out over the busy park and lake. People were strolling out in the peach haze of the evening sun and overweight birds with tatty feathers were gathering by the edge of the pond for their last feed of white sliced and crisps. I heard a child clacking a piece of wood along the iron railings. He stopped and walked around someone in his way, a man in a yellow, peaked baseball cap pulled down over his eyes, a white sleeveless vest and slightly baggy jeans. He was resting his back against the bars, lean coffee-coloured arms folded over his chest, one leg stretched out, one leg bent. I stared down at him until my gaze willed his head up to look at the window. He smiled and tipped his hat at me. Warren. What a nerve. What a nerve that man had.

I ran out of the room to the hall and called through the open door. 'Richard. You go. I'll see you later.'

He dropped his hands by his sides and groaned. He protested and stood his ground.

'I've just seen someone I know. Got to sort something out. See you later,' I said.

'Look, if that bloke is outside, I'm going to go out and kick the living crap out of him. Don't be a prat, George.'

'It's not him. I promise you. It's someone I haven't seen in ages. Really . . . He's coming up the road.'

Richard still wouldn't budge. He looked at me suspiciously.

'Go on, Richard. Have a nice time. Please. He's a friend. Really,' I said.

His shoulders relaxed and he nodded at me before pulling the door shut. As soon as it was closed, I ran to the front room and watched Warren. He was watching Richard and when he was satisfied, he looked up at me.

He stared, arms folded and I stared back, arms folded. He wasn't shifting. In fact, he gave me a little wave. That was it. I hurried to the door, opened it, stamped down the steps and across the road. I was walking on steel springs, long even strides to where he was. My arm was swinging back even before I had stopped. It was coming forward with some force when I did, but Warren's lazy hand caught my wrist and held it firm. He smiled, dark lips over perfect teeth, hazel eyes glinting from under his hat. He was laughing at me.

'Temper, temper,' he said.

I ripped my arm away, marched back across the road and up the steps.

He called across the street, still leaning back against the railings.

'Oi. Hold on, I got something for you.'

'I don't want it.'

'Oh yes, you do, gel.'

'Oh no, I don't, boy.'

He sniggered into his chest and looked up. 'Oh yes, you do, gel.'

I went in and slammed the door, waiting breathlessly behind it, cursing and cursing until I felt calmer. Then I walked into the lounge and over to the window. He was still there. He knew I couldn't resist. I swore again, walked back, opened the door and yelled across the street.

'Come on, then. Show me.'

Warren tipped at his hat, pushed himself off the railings and loped across towards me, his hands stuck deep in his pockets.

'Nice. Very nice,' he said, looking around the place.

I didn't answer.

'You doin' all right, then?'

'What do you want?' I said.

'Hey, come on. Be nice.'

'Why should I?'

'It's been a while, babe, that's why.'

I picked open my bag for my cigarettes. He watched me light up.

'Thought you'd have given them things up. Thing to do, innit?'

I inhaled deeply and flicked hard and repeatedly at the filter.

He tried again 'You're looking all right.'

'Thanks.'

'Bit pale. Don't you never go out in the sun?'

I crossed my arms over my chest and gripped my elbows. What a nerve.

'That guy that came out looks . . .'

'Warren, cut the crap. What've you got?'

He stopped smiling momentarily and then brightened again. 'I got something for you.'

'So you said. What?'

'Let's talk first.'

'Oh, fuck off.'

No one said anything for a hell of a long time. I spoke first this time.

'Your money's in the bank,' I said.

He frowned, then it registered. 'Ain't mine.'

'Well, it isn't mine.'

'Not took nothing?'

'Some, but I put it back.'

He shrugged and pointed at my dark glasses. 'You gonna take those things off?'

'No.'

He pushed his hat back a bit and wiped the sweat from under his nose. His pock-marked face was shiny with perspiration. 'Warm, innit?'

I thought I should throw him out. But I didn't. I wanted a drink and when I left the room for the kitchen, he followed me, waiting patiently as I grudgingly offered him a can of lager from the fridge and kept one for myself. His long fingers burst the seal on the can with a sharp little fizz. He took a long swallow, gasped, wiped his mouth and took a good look around. He pointed the can at the large, immaculate kitchen.

'This ain't you, babe, surely?'

I looked. There was a large well-stocked fridge-freezer. A double oven and a large pole from which hung shiny copper pans and two types of wok. There was a string of garlic on a butcher's hook and a row of herbs in neat pots on the window sill. The large wooden table was scrubbed clean, and there was no washing-up in the sink. Along one wall were shelves and shelves of cookery books. I tried not to laugh but the giggle in my throat crept out.

'No, Warren. This definitely ain't me.'

We stood drinking by the edge of the table as the sun went down. Then I took the crushed empty from his hand and dropped it in the bin.

'All right. What have you got?'

He pulled a 3.5-inch disk from his back pocket.

'Got a machine?' he said.

'Does Lassie have dog's breath?' I said, already walking down the hall to my room.

When I opened the door, his face glowed like he'd found a forgotten fiver. Compared to the rest of the house, it was a pit. Not as much of a pit as I could make it if I really put my mind to it. But, with Richard wandering in from time to time, I felt I had to make an effort. It was also a room for a single person, but I didn't think Warren would be bothered about that any more. He took the seat in front of the computer.

'I need a Pony. Gawd knows why they called it that. These Yanks don't understand nothing. Nor the Japs. Remember that kit they brought out called My Tool?' he said.

My computer was an IBM PC compatible. It didn't accept disks or software that ran on a Pony, which was designed for games and showed you little icon pictures, instead of hard-assed text commands, to help you move around the system. I walked over to the corner of the room and hunted through a huge pile of cartons until I came to the right shape.

'Here, next to the old Sinclair. It's been on test for three years.'

Warren unpacked the boxy little machine and set the thing up on what little space there was on my desk. I didn't watch the screen. I watched him. He was looking good, the same except his hair was shaved high over his ears and stylishly shaped to the nape of his neck. The top of his hat bore a roulette wheel design with 'Las Vegas' stamped across it. I could see the label inside his plain white vest. It said Calvin Klein.

The machine came alive as fresh and keen as if I'd bought it yesterday. Warren slotted the disk into the Pony's drive and turned to me.

'Now, look, I'm gonna run this but don't shoot the messenger, like. All right?'

'Get on with it.'

He sighed and his long quick fingers tapped at the buttons on the mouse pointer. A sequence of pictures in black and white appeared on the screen. Slowly, I put my hands to my face in horror. There was a woman gyrating in crotchless knickers and a nippleless bra. She smiled and the screen moved down her body. I yelled at Warren and pushed him aside, putting my one hand on the screen and hitting the keyboard with the other. The program disappeared.

'Where did you get that?'

'Look, I said don't shoot the messenger. I can see it ain't you.'

'You bet it isn't.'

53

'I know it ain't.' He sounded panicky.

'I know it isn't me. How do you bloody well know?' I said, snatching the glasses from my eyes and staring at him. He looked shocked.

'Well . . .'

'What?'

'Well . . . from what I can remember, um, looking at you now . . . you ain't that big . . . you know, up top . . .'

'Oh, Christ, don't . . .'

I leaned on the desk, squeezing my forehead with my hand until he took my chin and pulled my head gently around. His hand tugged at the tight collar around my neck and his eyes looked watery and sad.

'What kind of trouble you in now, George?' he said.

CHAPTER SIX

I couldn't tell him everything. I didn't trust him enough to tell him about me and David Jones. So I told him nothing. He didn't tell me a whole lot either. I did ask him how come he wasn't in jail but he just laughed and asked how come I wasn't dead yet. Under the circumstances, it wasn't very funny. I flopped back on the bed, my legs dangling off the edge. He sat at my desk.

'How did you find me?' I said.

'Every move you make, every step you take . . . I've been watching you . . .' Mercifully, he couldn't remember much more of the song.

'Come on.'

'I phoned your mother.'

'You what?'

'Your father answered the phone.'

'I don't believe this.'

'He remembered me. Quite friendly, he was. You never told 'im, then?'

'Would you tell your parents?'

'Yeah, well. They said, would you call.'

'Then they gave you this number.'

'Right. Don't look like that. They didn't do nothing wrong. I said it was important.'

Warren didn't seem to know what to do with his hands. I wasn't making anything easy for him. He pursed his lips together as if he wanted to whistle but thought better of it and blew out in a long frustrated sigh. 'You working on a story, then?' he said.

'Tell me how you got that thing,' I said.

'I won it.'

I propped myself up. 'You won it?'

'Yep.'

'Competition?'

'Sort of.' He looked away and played about with the keyboard.

'Warren.'

'In a SIG game. Pony users only,' he said.

Like the military, the computer business is very big on TLAs. Three Letter Abbreviations. SIG means Special Interest Group and that's what it is, a group of people with a special interest. A club. You get a lot of SIGs within computer-user associations and computer clubs. You also get them on videotex information systems like Prestel, electronic mail systems and computer hobbyists' bulletin boards. My story on computer porn had begun with computer buffs of a tender age downloading porn programs from the latter. The SIG operated in closed conference, scrambled so no uninvited eyes could see what came onscreen and no one could log on without alerting the group. Maybe someone was getting back at me for spoiling their fun.

'So what are you doing here with your little prize? Gloating?' I said.

I didn't really think he was but he was an available pin-cushion. He feigned wounded feelings.

'I didn't like it. Thought maybe if you saw it, you might know who would want to set you up like that.'

'That's all?'

'Yeah, so do you?'

'No. But I might know why.'

I told him about the porn story that had run in *Technology Week* and had been picked up by the

Sundays. He said he hadn't seen the story. I got a bad feeling about him again. I didn't trust Warren. Well, why should I? He'd said he loved me, and then damned near got me arrested by leaving me a whole load of money that he'd got by very devious means indeed. Arrested, nothing, he damned near got me killed.

'How come you didn't see the story?' I said.

'I just got back.'

'From where?'

'Las Vegas.'

Of course, the hat. Warren in Las Vegas. The idea of it created pictures that didn't fit. Warren was a London boy, an ex-London cabbie, an ex-British Telecom engineer. Warren was Las Palmas. Warren was not Las Vegas. Las Vegas was polyester slacks, dated shows with dancing rhinestone cowboys and bare-breasted snow queens. Still, with the money he had made, Warren could be anything he damn well wanted.

'You won me in Las Vegas? What do you do there?'

'Play games.'

'Do you ever. At the tables?'

He looked at me. Think again.

'Computer games?'

'Right,' he said.

'Holiday?'

He shook his head. Work then. Well, well.

'Security.'

'Had to be,' I said, more to myself than him.

I took two mugs of coffee into the front room and looked for a place to put them. Warren wouldn't keep still. He kept walking round, picking things up, putting them down, picking them up again.

'You live with this bloke, then?'

'What's it to you?' I said, clearing newspapers from the wooden coffee table, being careful to tuck coasters underneath. 'Richard is my landlord. Here, and don't mark the furniture.'

He took the coffee and looked out of the window over the park. He was picking up personal details too.

'Nice,' he said. 'You gave the flat back then?'

'Yes. It went to the next person on the list. Why, do you need it?'

I knew he didn't. Why fly in from Las Vegas in a Calvin Klein vest and chic, sheared hair to pick up the keys to a low-rent housing association flat in Bow?

'Nah,' he said, turning around and looking at me.

I didn't sit down either. 'Why'd you come back, Warren?' I said.

He looked out of the window again. 'Told ya. To show you the program.'

'All the way from Las Vegas?'

'It's not that far.'

'It's not cheap. You could have posted it.'

Warren put the mug down carefully on the coaster. Then he was back looking out of the window. 'Your bloke do that to you?'

My hand went defensively to my neck. He turned his back on the window and took off his hat. The top of his head squirmed with short corkscrew toggles as he rubbed his hand back and forth through them. I didn't answer, Warren answered for me.

'You're right, it ain't nothin' to do with me.'

'Correct.'

'So, you still drinking?' he said.

'I'm still drinking, Warren. You still nagging?'

I looked around for a packet of cigarettes that I thought I'd left in the room. I caught sight of them on the dresser and indicated to him. He brought them over to the chair where I was sitting, with an ashtray and a box of matches. I nodded, tapped one out and lit up.

'Still screwing around?' he said.

I looked up and took the cigarette from my mouth. 'You bastard.'

'I'm sorry, I shouldn't . . .'

'So what if I am? You still hacking? Still stealing? Still selling out your friends?'

'I never sold you out.'

'You bloody well did.'

'Saw you all right.'

'Sure.'

'You never understood nothing, girl.'

'What did you bring me the program for, Warren?'

'I told you, I won it. In Vegas. Thought you might like to know.'

'Why didn't you just keep it? Get off on it?'

'I don't get off on that shit.'

'Don't tell me. You care.'

'All right, I won't. I don't.'

He dumped himself in Richard's capacious sofa. I smoked. He smouldered. Same old Warren, but now that he was here and we had had our digs, it wasn't so bad. I had to be careful. It would be easy for me to take everything out on him. I ought to be nicer. After all, he'd come all the way from Las Vegas to bring me a present. Some women get personalized silk underwear. I get personalized porn.

'Do you still love me, Warren?' I said.

He pushed himself backwards, deep into the sofa and folded his arms tight over his chest.

'Nah,' he said. 'I got more bleeding sense.'

There was a Jiffy bag with my mail in the hall. Richard had picked the lot up and stacked them in the wire basket I kept by the door. I didn't recognize the handwriting but I guessed who it would be from. There was a disk inside but no note. I flicked through the rest of the mail, picked out three more envelopes which looked as if they bore cheques and took them and the disk from Julie Went-worth back to my bedroom.

I sat at my desk, powered up my machine and shoved the disk in the slot. His and her porno disks. I'd seen hers, now for his. The directory showed just one file – Killjoy – and I didn't stop to think any more, I just ran it.

It was David all right, from the back, waist up, and there was a naked woman strapped to what appeared to be a vertical pallet. The action was quick. He took two horizontal swipes across her body and the blood pumped from her wounds. He took another swipe, turned and walked away. His perspiring face was set with determination, and he came relentlessly towards me until his chest filled the screen. From the purple stripe twisted around my neck, the bloody stains in my eyes and the sick feeling in my stomach, I knew that this program could be the real thing. Unless I was the real thing and this was the fake, a signal for how he wanted it to be.

I sat for a while in my room just pushing a pencil through my fingers. If David had created the two sequences his wife had shown me, then it wasn't too hard to attribute the one Warren had brought me to him as well. If David had created all three, whether fake or real, he was probably involved in the game Warren had played.

I picked up the phone and dialled an old familiar number.

A soft companionable voice replied. 'Computer Section. Inspector Falk speaking.'

'Robert? It's Georgina.'

'Mrs Powers. What a delightful surprise. What can I do for you?'

'I've received something through the post. It's to do with the porn story. Can you look something up for me?'

'Of course. What?'

'A possible missing person.'

'Mmm. All right.'

'Thanks. Anything I can do for you?'

'Seen anyone lately?'

'What do you mean?'

'Just wondered.'

'Why?'

'Warren Graham's back in town.'

'Oh, him.'

'Yes, him.'

'He's been here. Bet you knew when he'd arrived, huh?'

'Bet your life.'

I didn't want the conversation to go much further because I couldn't lie to Robert. I had to leave things out. He knew that. He did the same thing, told the truth to me, in manageable pieces.

We'd become friends in the middle of a great computer scam that had netted Warren a great deal of money but had been so embarrassing for all concerned that they let him go. They never caught him anyway. Robert was the policeman on the spot and he had had to swallow his pride, just like I had. At least Warren had left me a little place to live and some money. He'd left Robert Falk with egg all over his huge face.

There was no word from David. The days got hotter and I began to feel that maybe it would be better if I looked after Number One and stayed out of it. Let Mrs Jones take care of him. As for Warren, he was beginning to live his song. He was watching me. It seemed that every time I popped out of the house, he'd be walking up the road, or about to ring the bell, calling me up just before I left the house, just passing *Technology Week*'s offices when I went in there. He'd given me a number to call if I wanted to get in touch, but he never gave me time to miss him.

To tell the truth, I was beginning to like having him around again.

'How long are you over here for?' I said, passing him a pint and moving away from the bar to stand out on a shady part of the crowded pavement.

'Long as I like,' he said, putting his arm out protectively as someone stepped back into me. I waited for his arm to drop, and wiped the froth from my top lip. The lager was cold and hurt my teeth.

'Does that mean you haven't got a job?' I said.

'It means I'm freelance, like you. Great, innit?'

'T'rific.'

The sun was high and bright but the haze of the city smudged its rays and yellowed the blue sky. I could see myself reflected in Warren's beetle-black glasses, bug-eyed in my own. I wanted to peel away his skull and climb in, find out how much he knew and why he was pussyfooting around. Perhaps if I gave him a bit more, he might tell. If I didn't know better, I'd give him one more chance.

'I think I've worked out where whoever faked that program videoed my face,' I said. Warren's black-lensed eyes looked blankly at me.

'Yeah?'

'Yes. I was at an exhibition not long ago. I'm sure it was there. I lost an earring there. One earring. If you look at it, you'll find that's all the bit that's me is wearing.'

'You didn't notice nothing? No one about?'

'Nope,' I lied.

'Didn't notice when you lost it?'

'Nope.' The truth.

David had stood in the hall across from me. You could put a video stills camera in your pocket. It figured. He could have done it there. It would have been easy. I wanted Warren to tell me about the game. See if I could put the pieces of this story together.

'How long you reckon to get a list?' he said.

Good question. I told him, I'd got a list of exhibitors.

'Visitors?'

Smart.

'The organizers might have got it together by now. Have to push a bit to get that. They'll be using that as a commodity now, mailing lists for business, you know.'

'If I were you, I'd get it. Maybe you'll log a name, maybe I will. 'Nother drink?'

He'd taken my glass before I could answer and was pushing his way back into the pub. I looked straight ahead across the road and smiled to myself until I saw David, slim, spare and suited, looking right back. I stepped backwards and then started to move towards him. I stopped, ashamed of myself, of the hammering heart in my chest. He had one hand in his pocket and a slim metal briefcase in the other. He looked cool, clean and smart. I lifted my hand to my throat and then up, waving weakly. Thank God he couldn't see my eyes. I smiled a little, but he didn't. He just nodded, turned and walked away.

I leaned my back on the wall for support, my legs buckling under me, and someone said: 'Hi.'

It was Diane. Big smile, white teeth. She had a fruit juice in one hand and Richard on the other, a pint of best bitter in his hand. I straightened up.

'Oh hi,' I said.

'On your own?'

'I'm waiting for someone.'

'You don't look very well, you all right?'

'PMT,' I replied. Another TLA. TLL. Another Tiny Little Lie.

'Poor you.'

I pushed my glasses tighter against my head and Diane looked around.

I looked at Richard, who was looking at me rather too closely, but before I could answer Warren walked out of the pub with our drinks. Diane looked quickly at me and then at Warren, a big grin over her face, her fine dark eyebrows lifting. Warren produced a big, silly grin too. Diane did that to men.

'Warren Graham. Diane Shine. Richard Munroe,' I said without enthusiasm and everyone nodded at everyone else, Richard with more suspicion than the others, and they all said hello. As soon as Warren opened his mouth to speak, Richard's face tightened up.

'Don't I know you?' he said. Diane looked at Richard, surprised at his tone.

Warren shook his head, his face betraying nothing. 'No, mate, not me.'

'On the telephone. You called while we were having dinner.' Richard made it sound like a hanging offence.

Warren just smiled. 'Sorry 'bout that. You didn't say. Would've called back, know what I mean?'

I hoped Richard wasn't going to be misled by the cheerful cockney chappie routine. I tapped Richard on the arm.

'Don't push it, Richard, please. I told you. It's not him.'

Richard broadened his shoulders, confident that his experience on the rugby field and in the occasional pitched battle in the clubroom would intimidate the smaller man with the lippy look. He was very much a fist man, you could see that. But I'd seen Warren with a knife once, and he'd always carried a cosh under the seat in his cab: a whole different ballgame, as they say. Warren pushed his glasses up his nose and Richard nodded sharply and gave way, steering Diane off the pavement to another part of the crowd. I could see her talking angrily to him.

Warren took a good sup from his pint. 'Friendly sort, your landlord.'

'He is as a rule. But he thinks you're someone else.'

Warren touched my neck lightly with a cool finger. 'Thinks I did this, yeah?'

'Yes.'

'Thinks I fit the part, yeah? Black, pig ignorant, pimp type, yeah?'

'Don't be silly, they wear huge suits and lots of gold.'

'Maybe mah girls ain't that good, baby momma.' He laughed, pumping his shoulders up and down, and then stood ramrod straight, finger straight under his nose. 'Don't like the cut of your jib, old chap. How long have you been beating this young gel?'

I told him to shut up. He was beginning to get on my nerves. I glanced anxiously across the road again and down the street.

Warren kept on. He had a point to make. 'My guess. Let me guess. This geezer, the one you won't let on about, the one who knocks you about, you know. My guess is he's one of them smart, white, middle-class nut-nuts. He's got a suit, a good job, maybe in computers, soft hands, specs, the quiet, polite type. So fucking respectable, and so full of shit.'

I screamed at him to stop and silenced the drinkers on the street. Warren stopped all right and grabbed me.

I pushed his hands off and ran up the street. He called my name and tried to run after me but as I rounded the corner, I saw Richard ground him with a crushing tackle.

CHAPTER SEVEN

'Who was that man?' David said.

'Who?' I knew who.

'The black man.'

'A friend,' I said.

'Do you sleep with him?'

'No. Why?'

'I was watching you.'

'Are you jealous?'

'Not at all.'

'Good.'

'I can't see you this week.'

'So what? It's over,' I said.

'Why?' His voice was dry, unconcerned, enough to make me feel afraid.

'You know why.'

'We were in control.'

'You were.'

'Trust me.'

'I don't.'

'Don't worry, I can shield you.'

'From what?'

'From myself.'

I put the phone down in the cradle.

Warren spoke, breaking the silence that hung heavily in the room. He was lying back on my bed, arms tucked behind his head. 'Should've told the bastard to shove it.'

I turned away from my desk, pushed a few papers here and there and changed the subject. I wished Warren had left the room. He wanted to listen and pick up clues that I didn't want him to have. He felt sorry for me. I knew it, and I didn't like it either. I'd always thought that if we ever met again, I'd show him up. He'd be no more than a rootless fugitive crushed by guilt and haunted by the past. I'd fought for truth and justice and so I'd be the one shining with health, success and untroubled by regret. Life's a bitch.

'How was Richard with you when you arrived?' I said.

'OK. Didn't say much. He was late for work.'

'He has been every day this week. His leg's giving him gyp.'

'He was in a right state.'

'I notice you're still not shaving.'

Warren had a scabby trail down one side of his face and his left arm. It made him look rough in spite of the expensive cream sweatshirt he was wearing. A heavy gold chain twinkled round his neck and another thicker band, plain with no initials, shone from his wrist. East End boys liked to have markers of their success, preferably not less than 18 carat. Warren was no different, but at least he'd kept it simple.

I was sure that he knew people were watching him. That's why I hadn't bothered to mention that DI Robert Falk had noted his whereabouts. I didn't think it would be news or, if it was, that it would bother him much. He must have had every corner covered to turn up in this city after this time just to look up an old friend, who might or might not be a friend at all. He seemed untroubled by his past, more confident and arrogant than ever. He'd made fools of us all, and fools quickly turn to enemies. We were all waiting, waiting for him to make that one mistake, so we could crow and crow. At least I thought that I had been waiting just like all the rest, but here he was again, lying back, nice and comfy, on my bed. A small tremor of doubt tickled my mind. If he had so much cash, why did he need a job in casino security to pay his bills? I'd save that one for later.

Meanwhile, poor Richard wasn't impressed by him at all. Warren was a dirty fighter, he said, and Diane made out she wasn't impressed by either of them. She didn't keep Richard in the doghouse for long, though. She patted his head and he lapped it up. They both interrogated me, wanting to know what had got into me, why I'd run howling down the street.

Warren didn't ask. He came round with flowers. 'I'm really sorry,' he had said.

'Yes, well.'

'I wanted you to tell me who it was.'

'So you told me instead.'

'Yeah, I know.'

'You saw him, didn't you? I thought you were inside the pub.'

'I was. I watched through the door.'

'Why bother, Warren?'

He didn't answer me. He watched me unwrap the stiff paper from around the bright, summer blooms in silence, waiting as I opened and shut cupboards in search of a vase that would be big enough.

'Well?' I said, straightening up with something ornate and heavy in cut glass.

'If he's who I think he is, he's bad news.'

Tell me about it.

We went to my room where I had been working. Warren did what he never could resist doing. He straightened out my bed before lying back on it. I sat at my untidy desk in front of my personal computer.

'Tell me about it,' I said.

The way Warren told it, he'd been tooling around with the systems at The Dice Palace in Las Vegas, where he

68

worked. He didn't mention why he needed it, but he'd got the job monitoring the casino systems with a single reference. He was a technothief. He understood systems, networks and telecommunications and he understood cheats. When the job got really boring, which was most of the time, he logged on to national and international data networks just to see what was going on. One night he picked up a number for a bulletin board that was just for games players.

'Ever see a film called *Westworld*?'

'*Westworld*? The sci-fi?'

'Yeah. Punters travel to this futuristic Disneyland. They pick which worlds they want to spend their holiday in. Romanworld, Futureworld, Westworld. Right?'

'Right.'

'They can do what they like because all the so-called people there are robots. So in Westworld you dress up as cowboys and take on the gunslinger . . .'

'Yul Brynner.'

'Do him over and over again. He's just a machine. And you can screw the girlie robots as much as you like, rape and pillage, do what you like.'

'Sounds like Butlin's.'

'I found a game called Pornoland, I think your man was in it.'

What Warren then described was a typical adventure game of the type that anyone could play on a home computer. Unlike the shoot-'em-up or race circuit varieties, the aim of the game is not to test reflexes or manual dexterity, but tactics, strategy and imagination while playing a role in a fantastic world. Magic and mystery are the mainstays of these games, as they try to simulate the action of a fantasy novel from the viewpoint of the protagonists. The big attraction of role-playing games is that they are open-ended. They can last for hours, weeks, months, or even years.

The games can be played solo, but like cards they are much more fun with other players. One player takes the part of the referee or storyteller, while others assume the personae of different characters who then proceed through these digitized imaginary worlds, in search of some Holy Grail, destroying dragons and rescuing fair maidens along the way. Each character is defined in terms of strength, endurance, intelligence and whatever other talent might be needed in any particular scenario, and these characteristics can develop as the game proceeds. In a space game, there would be intergalactic traders, mercenaries, troopers and scouts of varying ability and morality to outwit. In a fantasy game, there would be legendary warriors, magicians, assassins and thieves. In a porno game: just plain pimps, whores, gangsters, police – and psychopaths, of course.

'What's the basic scenario?' I said.

'You start off in the mean streets and you have to reach the top. You got to avoid the villains, the filth and make a lot of money. You get points and you win prizes. Real prizes. Like you.'

'What if you lose?'

'You don't win points and you don't win prizes.'

'So how did you win me?'

'Level Four Pornoland.'

'Oh, how lovely. How?'

'I did your pimp. 500 points plus bonus. 1000 points.'

'Thank you.'

'Now you belong to me, girl.'

'No, I don't.'

He fell silent and looked up at the ceiling. Little beads of sweat had started to form on my top lip. I knew who he was thinking about.

'You belong to him, doncha?' he said.

'No.'

He didn't believe me, and I wasn't sure I believed it

myself. But if he wanted me to crack and cry out my troubles he'd forgotten too much about me. I had more questions to ask him anyway.

'They wouldn't let just anyone play that game, would they? Just dialling in?' I said.

'Nah.'

'So?'

'You start playing on another bulletin board. A games one. I played this Dungeons and Dragons thing. I had this great score but I got stuck trying to free the princess who was tied to the Traitor's Gate.'

'Don't tell me, she had the body of Wonderwoman and the brains of Snow White.'

'Listen, will you? The water was rising, time was running out, if I didn't do something we'd both drown, I'd lose all me points and be back at square one.'

'Oh heavens!' I said, throwing up my hands in mock horror. 'Warren, what did you do?'

'I said, fuck the girl, I'm getting out of here.'

'Bastard. What did you really do?' I said.

'That's what I really did.'

'So you lost?'

'As it happens, that was the right answer. Up comes a message saying blah-de-blah you're right, there was no solution, but your nasty mind gets you into another world. Call this number. Strictly payment by credit card.'

'Pornoland.'

'Yeah.'

'How far does it go?'

'Very tacky.'

'How far?'

'Makes Caligula look like that bleeding frog, Kermit.'

'Kids?'

'Yeah.'

'Snuff?'

'The lot.'

71

There were those champagne bubbles again, tickling the news buds under my tongue. I was actually salivating.

'So what logo do you get when you log in?' I said.

'For the games? JJ 1000.'

'JJ 1000?'

'Yeah.'

'So who's JJ?' I said.

'Dunno.' I had a pretty good idea what it meant. JJ could only stand for Julie Jones. People liked to use their loved ones' initials for passwords and all sorts.

'What do you get the next time?'

'Nothing. You get asked for your credit card number and told that you need a Pony because the graphics won't work otherwise.'

'So what do you see, graphics, text?'

'Both. Graphics for the scenery. Text instructions and storyline. You get to choose what character you want from scanned photos. They come up on the screen right at the start.'

'Don't tell me you get complete motion video too?'

'Nah, the machines aren't that powerful and the comms isn't that reliable. Just plain ordinary graphics will slow games up. You know, takes for ever for the figures to get across a screen from A to B. I told you, text, photos and a bit of graphics thrown in when you got to see something to believe it.'

'And are the graphics good?'

Warren's face didn't alter much but his wicked hazel eyes did. A small smile was developing.

'They ain't half bad.'

'Oh, go on.'

He looked a little crestfallen. I had a horrible suspicion that he had wanted to talk dirty.

'Go on!'

'The game uses the graphics figures for secondary characters, ones that are always part of the game and that turn up along the way. They aren't players. Some of these secondary figures are derived from photos. Get it?'

'The players call in and choose from the photos.'

'Yeah. But you do get a little graphical representation of that player too. It's very basic VR, see. You're working the strings on yourself in a different world.'

'Virtual reality?'

'Yeah. Course, without the sensory deprivation. OK, the VR extras, the data gloves and helmets, are about, but they're not cheap enough to distribute for games machines. When they are, you'll feel as if you're actually in there. There's stuff like that around, you know.'

'I know.'

I didn't want to tell him that I had had personal coaching on the subject by the world's number one. If I started to tell him that, I'd want to tell him more. In the meantime, Warren had a lot to tell me.

'So where did I come in?' I said.

'Little pre-set sequences of video stills that run together are offered as little prizes. Sometimes they're part of the game.'

'The characters shake hands, I suppose.'

'Sometimes, but mostly . . .'

'I was joking, Warren. So the good news is I was in the photo line-up?'

'No.'

'I thought you said people could dial in and choose a character from a photo line-up?'

'They can. He was in the line-up. But you weren't. You're just a secondary character to work with. You were just an option.'

'So how far did you get?'

'I told you. I won.'

I looked away and Warren didn't say any more. He rolled over, picked up my cigarettes from the clutter on my bedside table, played around with the packet and

73

then flicked it open. He offered, I took one. He took my cheap petrol-blue lighter and flicked up a flame. He tried not to look into my eyes, but I was chasing him, daring him. Warren was good enough to work out the cheats in any game. He'd have had his tastes satisfied. The ones we'd never explored in real life back there in Bow.

'What's your problem then, Warren?' I said.

'Don't get you.'

'Why'd you play?'

He tilted his head and looked at me from under his eyebrows, the smile broadening on his dark lips. 'Because it was there, babe, just because it was there.'

I took a couple of drags and filled the room with fresh smoke. Bullshit. Warren had recognized David Jones. From the game. Bad news, he'd said, but he hadn't got a name. JJ 1000 hadn't meant anything to him. Warren hadn't mentioned any names that mattered, yet.

'I got to the desktop,' he said.

I'd been waiting for it. He would not have been able to resist finding out a little more about his whereabouts beyond the game. He had got out of the computer playground and into the computer operating system, which meant he could browse around the games machine and see what else was there. If he wanted to, he could play a few tricks on the bulletin board owner and get a free ride over the system.

'What did you find out?' I said.

'It had some new games that hadn't run yet on the games board. Not bad at all. It had some comms software . . .' He hesitated for a moment, as if he were having second thoughts.

'And? Did you use it?'

''Course I did.'

'And?'

'Called a number. Read the mail.'

'Come on, Warren.'

'There were some messages there from some geezer called David. Familiar? He stayed in town a hell of a lot.'

I kept cool. If he wasn't going to say anything, neither was I. Warren had seen him across the street, he'd said. Only because I had suggested it. Now, he was saying he'd seen him in the game, seen his name in a mail message. Lies, then the truth, telling me what I wanted to hear. That was all.

'So you think he's the same guy?' I said.

'Yeah, he's the one. David. Don't shit me. He's your bloke, ain't he? He the geezer across the street?'

'His name is David Jones, Warren. His wife's name is Julie Jones. Get it? That's your JJ 1000. Forget the wife, she's a victim too. He's the man, Warren. He's the man.'

Julie Wentworth never liked to talk on the phone. She always wanted to see me, face to face. Maybe she had no friends.

'What's happening?' she said.

I didn't like to tell her about the program Warren had won nor that he had read her mail. I wanted to ask her about JJ 1000 first and the entertainment option on the Jones family machine.

'Not much,' I said. She blew out her cheeks and sighed.

'Have you spoken to him about it at all?' I said.

'Yes, I said I'd seen the one of me.'

'And what did he say?'

'He said I wouldn't do it, so he made me do it himself.'

That sounded like David. Another easy matter-of-fact explanation without any irksome morals cluttering up the place.

'Did he ask if you'd seen any more?' I said.

'Yes. I said no, but I'd like to see any that he had. He said no.'

'Didn't he say anything else? Wasn't he shocked or surprised?'

'No. That's not him. He said that's what computers were for.'

'What?'

'To replace jobs humans found a chore.'

'Oh, charming.'

'There's more, Georgina. I think he has another woman. I'm sure he has.'

She touched my arm with her soft hand when she said this. It was a peculiar feeling, as if she trusted me. I felt guilty. I wondered how warm the skin, where her fingers had pressed, felt to her. I felt red hot. My pulse was beating like a signal, a secret beacon in a dark sea. She had caught me out again. I tried to avoid her eyes, hide my surprise.

'I know what you're thinking. Why should that bother me after all this?' she said, getting it all wrong.

'It had crossed my mind,' I said.

'He's my husband.'

'Of course.'

'And what if, you know . . .'

'What?'

'What if he sets her up like the woman on that disk?' she said. She was looking tearful again. Her rodent eyes were all wet and glassy. I felt the tickle of fear begin.

'You don't think it's a fake then? It could be, you know. The others are,' I said.

'Others?'

I took a drink while she looked intently at me. You idiot, I said to myself.

'I mean the one of you. I presume he's made others.'

'Yes, maybe, but what if some are real? The one I sent you. What if it's real? What if he really killed her? He wants to do it, doesn't he? He wants to kill a woman. Who'd make up a thing like that if they didn't really want to do it? What if this woman he's seeing is another one, another victim? I have to do something. You must help me.'

I picked open a packet of cigarettes and lit up. I couldn't put my hand on her arm to ease her fears. I wasn't sure what to do for the best. I had myself to think about, the marks of his hands only just fading from my throat.

'People's fantasies are often just that, you know, fantasies,' I said.

Her reply was contemptuous. 'Fantasies? Fantasies are supposed to be in your head.'

'Not always. We have literature, we have art.'

'We have pornography.'

Did we ever, I thought, sticking my nose in my glass. I took my time, had a sip, had a drag on the ciggie, calmed myself. I had to sound nonchalant.

'Look, do you know anything about her, this other woman?' I said.

She wiped her tearless eye and fiddled with the stem of her glass. 'No. He stays in town. I know that. He doesn't have to stay over, but he does.'

'That doesn't mean anything,' I lied.

'I can't stand it.'

There was anguish in her voice. She loved him, still, and I knew then that she would protect him no matter what, if only he loved her. That was the only price. He could rape and murder, gouge and mutilate, provided he came home to her with love and respect. The infinite forgiveness she had to give would fall like soft rain to wash clean his sins. He could do it to them as long as he still loved her but I didn't think he did. I wondered what she might do when she found out that he didn't. My wife will kill me, he had said.

'You look better,' she said, wiping away real tears now.

'Oh?'

'I didn't like to say, but you looked very poorly when we met last.'

'I had a bit of an accident,' I lied.

'I think he knows I've been to see you,' she said.

'How?' I said, sweat gathering under my arms.

'Maybe after I told him, he started watching me.'

I put down the glass and placed my hand comfortingly on her cool tanned arm. I had to take a risk now, let her step a little closer to protect myself. I told her about the game, hating myself for the sympathetic tones I introduced to my voice, like cheap veneer brightening a familiar surface of old wood. I didn't tell her about the charming little sequence of me. I didn't want her to ask why I should be performing in what we assumed was David's electronic fleshpot. I just told her that the game included shots of real people and sequences of them in any number of compromising positions.

'It's definitely running on a Pony – or something compatible with it. Has David got one? It's a pretty distinctive machine.'

She didn't touch her drink. Her hands were pressed tightly together on her lap. I thought that maybe I should have waited for her to absorb the news about the game before thundering in about the whereabouts of the machine. She flushed when she started to speak.

'I'm not sure. I think so. I'm not that good with computers. Look, I'm not on this game, am I? He's not using me?'

'I don't think so. Really, I don't. He might have a copy of that disk, though. Probably has,' I said.

'Oh God.'

'How much do you know about computing – can you use a machine?'

'Word processing, that's about my limit.'

I made a mental note to ask Warren if he'd poked

around in anything she'd written. He hadn't said. I'd never asked.

'What do you do then?' I enquired.

She looked embarrassed. 'Oh, just a few letters. I'm a housewife, that's all. I did French at university, and that was that really after I met David.'

'Look, to get to the game you have to access a games bulletin board run under the logo JJ 1000,' I said.

'JJ. Julie Jones. That's me.'

I was trying to pressure her, just in case she was leaving anything out. She looked baffled and then her brain shifted gear.

'Look, am I going to get into bother about this? I mean, if he's using my name, if I use the same computer, how am I going to prove I'm innocent? What if the police come knocking, what could I say?'

I wasn't that worried about that. It was proving her husband guilty that was occupying my mind. Proving him guilty before he squeezed the life out of me, or her.

'Look, do you use a machine at home? Does he work from home?'

'Y . . . es, sometimes.'

'Where else?'

'The uni, sometimes.'

'Anywhere else?'

'What do you mean?'

'Does he work anywhere else?'

'Oh, the Science Park. You know that.'

I stopped. My face reddened under her gaze.

'What do you mean?' I said.

'You interviewed him, didn't you? Virtech Ltd. You interviewed him in New York.'

'Oh yes.'

'I bet you didn't think he was capable of this.'

'No,' I said, flicking my cigarette in the ashtray, avoiding her gaze. 'But then, we only talked business.'

I drained my glass and looked across to the bar. Warren was wiping raindrops off his jacket. The man was like a shadow. Julie looked around and followed my eyes. Warren saw us sitting by the door and gave a cheerful wave before walking over with a solitary pint of beer.

'Could do with the rain, eh, ladies? Can I get you a drink?'

Julie covered her glass with her hand and shook her head. I nodded firmly and Warren took my glass back to the bar.

'Warren's helping me on this story,' I said as we waited for him to come back. He sat down and I introduced her.

'Warren, Julie is David Jones's wife.'

I was ashamed to say it, but if he understood that, he didn't show it. He grinned amiably at her. She put out her hand and Warren took it in his long dark fingers. She looked directly at him, smiling a little stiffly all the while. I think she was embarrassed. I hadn't had time to tell her that Warren hadn't seen all the evidence. Nothing much was said after that and she seemed to want to leave. Despite the rain, Warren was able to call her a black cab through an old, reliable contact, and he chatted while she waited. She, for her part, seemed more at ease after he'd worked on her, delighting her with tall tales of his previous life driving round the streets of London. I never heard so many cor blimeys. The man deserved an Equity card.

'You finished?' I said when she'd gone.

He threw open his hands in innocence. 'What?'

'The crafty cockney routine. Bin it.'

'They love it. Anyway, I had to change the subject. What you expect me to say to her? I hear your husband's a raving nut-nut?'

'She's going to try and suss out her machine, see if there's anything there about JJ 1000.'

'Any idea what sort of phone he's using?' he replied, serious now, and peeved with me.

'I didn't ask, why?'

'Well, if it's hanging off a portable, it's going to be interesting trying to find it.'

'I'm assuming she uses the machine at home.'

'Yeah, but it don't have to stay there, does it? Think about it.'

I did. It had to be on a machine that she used if it had comms software on it that would help her dial out and pick up her mail. It was probably at their house, if she worked there, and I assumed that she did. But Warren was right. If anyone wanted to move it quickly and still keep it operational, a mobile phone was the thing. There was no reason why it couldn't be at Virtech. I should have asked if she worked there. While I made a mental note to give her a call, Warren took a sip from his chestnut-coloured beer and ran his pink tongue over the froth on his top lip. I tapped my last cigarette out of its packet. The smoke I pushed over our heads drifted down into the shiny, damp ringlets of his hair. He was looking good, better than me. I wasn't wearing as well but then, I hadn't been trying.

'No way she gonna do it,' he said.

'If it's on her machine and she knows her way around the directory, she could.'

'Look, even if it's staring her in the face, she won't get it. You seem to forget that computers are a fucking mystery to most people. It's an invisible option anyway, she won't see it unless she knows it's there. What she do?' he said.

I told him she was a housewife, with a French degree, who did a little secretarial work for the bread-winner.

'Kids?'

'What?'

'They got kids?'

81

'Are you deliberately trying to make me feel worse?'

'I only asked.'

Warren drank some more from his pint, licked his lips again and sat twiddling his hands between his legs. We didn't say much for a while.

'What's with the beer? It never was a great favourite of yours,' I said, emptying my glass.

'British, innit?'

'You missed the place, then?'

'Sometimes.'

'What did you miss?'

'The verbal. First week in New York and I couldn't get a glass of water anywhere. Couldn't understand me. Thought I was an Aborigine. I had to ask for fucking Perrier all the time.'

'How awful.'

'It got worse. Asked for Scotch and dry once and got Haig with a Martini in it.'

'What else?'

'What?'

'What else did you miss?'

'The weather. They don't have no weather in Vegas. They have air conditioning instead. Weather comes in three flavours: hot, hotter and fucking hot. But with air conditioning you can freeze your bollocks off inside a casino when it's 100 degrees in the street. Nice to see a bit of rain, I can tell you.'

Warren picked the glasses up and bought another round. I didn't offer to pay. I never had done when he was around. He was old-fashioned and didn't hold with women paying their way. He came back and lectured me about smoking. Old habits die hard.

CHAPTER EIGHT

Richard liked the story but he couldn't bring himself to show it, because of Warren, who was slouching against his desk, arms folded, looking lazily around the offices of *Technology Week*. He didn't seem to be listening to us. He had his eyes on Diane. After a while, he smiled and gave her a little wave. She lit up like some illuminated Black Madonna, and coyly looked down at her work. Miss Wholesome.

'So you think it originates in this country?' Richard said.

'Yes.'

'Because of this phoney program of you?'

'Right, and because Warren here thinks so,' I said, but Richard didn't so much as turn his head. He looked at me and sucked at his teeth.

'Because Warren here thinks so? Oh, great.'

Warren turned his head towards us. 'The phone company told me,' he said quietly.

Richard turned to face him, folding his arms now, and tucking in his gut so that his shoulders and chest expanded like a farmyard cockerel's puffed-up ruff. 'How come?' he said.

'I asked,' was Warren's dry reply.

Richard turned back to me. 'Accessibility?'

'From anywhere on the right network if you've got a

Pony-compatible. Just dial in and give them your credit card number,' I said.

'How'd he get the number?'

'It was advertised on a bulletin board. JJ 1000.'

'What does BT know about it?'

'Nothing. Won't do anything unless the police tell it to. If it was running on one of its services, it'd just pull the plug. Under the Telecomms Act, it is an offence to transmit obscene material over the public telephone network.'

'That's it?'

'They're looking into it. I mean, the game isn't being transmitted, is it? People are dialling into it and it's not for public access, it's a closed user group. Any offence is in the transmission, not the reading of the stuff. They get round that by sending it scrambled. However, the system manager is leaving himself open to prosecution under the Obscene Publications Act, Cable and Broadcasting Act and the Telecommunications Act. We know that because of the last story.'

'So do you know who's running it?'

'I'm not sure but I've got an idea.'

'I want absolute proof before you implicate anyone, Georgina. OK. That's it. I'll talk to Max.'

'Of course. But no one else. Right?'

Warren had started fiddling about at Richard's desk, tapping here and there on the keyboard. Richard leaned over to him. 'Don't do that,' he said right in his face.

Warren looked up, eyeballed him and languidly stood up, moving his hand away. He waited a couple of seconds, with his thumbs casually tucked into his back pockets before moving off towards Diane. Richard stared after him like a man just wishing his hands were longer and stronger, then he turned back to me.

'Are you sure you can find out without letting the

operator know you're on to him? If he rumbles you, he'll close down the game and we won't have anything.'

'I think so. How's your leg today?' I asked.

'It's OK,' he said, looking over at Warren and Diane and then back at me. 'Are you sure you know what you're doing?' he whispered.

'What do you mean?'

'Hanging around with that bloke.'

He meant Warren.

'I told you. Warren brought me the information. He's a friend.'

'Yeah? Why the hell did you run away from him, then?'

'Ah well, Richard. Sometimes the truth hurts,' I said.

Warren had made himself comfortable on the side of Diane's desk now, laughing with her, lighting her up.

That night I was alone when David came to the door. I kept the chain on but I could see his pale eyes and straight mouth through the crack. I'd been drinking and I wished I hadn't. I'd been drinking because it's what I like to do especially when I need to talk to myself. At first, I wouldn't open the door but I couldn't shut it because he was leaning against it. I was afraid but as I stood staring at his unsmiling face, I felt driven like a hand drawing a thick black circle. The ends have to meet.

'Open the door,' he said.

'No.'

'I want to talk to you.'

'No.'

'It's about my wife.'

Guilt pushed me over the line and made me slip the chain. He pushed the door open gently and stepped in. The only sound in the house came from the television in the lounge.

'Who else is here?'

I could have said Richard was in his room but he would have known I was lying. So I said nothing but swept my arm down and bowed slightly as he walked past me along the hall.

'Let's go to your room,' he said.

'I don't want to do that.'

'I don't want to talk about this in a hallway.'

'The lounge then.'

'Someone might come in.'

'The lounge,' I said, walking in there so that he had to follow me. He switched off the box and I sat down on the sofa, motioning to the seat opposite. He stayed how he was, hands in his pockets, looking, to my inebriated mind, less composed than usual. Nevertheless, his tie was neat, his shirt white, his trousers uncreased. Sometimes he reminded me of an alien who had decided, through light years of study while travelling to earth, that this was a suitable disguise for an unremarkable existence in human society. The diamond pin that fired in the light gave him away. It displayed the peculiarly human trait of vanity.

'Drink?' I said.

I stared one-eyed down the neck of the quarter-full bottle and then pointed it at a handsome tallboy in the corner where there was a bottle of gin, a bottle of Scotch and some brandy on a tray. He didn't move. I felt irritated by his presence. I'd been comfortable alone in the house, muttering to myself, working my way through the wine while learning how to transplant a fruit tree from a gardening programme. When he had been outside, I had been afraid but now that he was inside, I wasn't and I stepped over the mark straight away.

'Sit down, for Chrissakes,' I said, leaning back, glass in hand. He stared and sat down, smooth-trousered, legs apart, tipping his metal-rimmed glasses a little with one scrupulously scrubbed hand.

'Matches?' I said, throwing him a box. He didn't pick them up. He didn't say anything. I got up, switched on the television again and settled back on the sofa with my drink.

'You know what?' I said. 'You ought to see a psychiatrist.'

He took his time and then said: 'I have. Have you?'

'No, never.'

'I'm surprised.'

'I believe in self-help,' I said, pouring the rest of the bottle into my glass, which I brought to my lips and placed down again, unsampled. 'Did he say you were a psychopath?' I said.

There was no flicker of offence taken. I looked up and he dropped his eyes to look at the bottle. Then he smiled, keeping still and smug and icy while I pushed my luck right into the abyss.

'A touch schizoid was her analysis,' he said.

'What does that mean?'

'You want to know what my psychiatrist said?'

'I want to know what it means.'

'It means a lot of things. It means I'm egocentric, hypersensitive, unsociable, cold and unemotional.' He counted out the list on his fingers.

'Any fresh news?' I said.

'How about a desire for power and superiority?'

'We know that.'

'Want to know why?'

I shrugged indifferently and picked my glass up again.

'I desire power and superiority to protect myself from emotional dependency, a necessary constituent in any intimate relationship, which, of course, I subconsciously crave but regard as too dangerous to contemplate.'

'Ahhhh. You just want to be loved. What about your wife? No intimacy there?' I said, holding the glass to me before lifting it to my lips and tipping it up. His face was distorted by the cheap lens it provided, smeared and foggy from my breath and fingertips. He still looked calm.

'Of course. I'm telling you what my psychiatrist says.'

'Oh. So what if you don't get what you want? Trouble, huh?'

'That's right.'

'Did she have any good news?'

'I can sublimate the aggression that I find difficult to release – most of the time.'

'Into what?'

'My work.'

'Well, hell, let's pray you don't get the push.'

He laughed at this point. Not a belly laugh or anything like that, a derisory sort of chuckle. It was encouraging, but I was losing confidence, like a bullet-ridden flier struggling to keep conscious and alive. I rested my head back on Richard's soft sofa and closed my eyes for a moment. I wanted to look through my warm red lids and forget he was there. He was enjoying himself, showing off. He moved to make himself more comfortable and I opened my eyes fast. He was in the same safe place, across the room from me, stroking his smooth hands over the rounded velvety arm of the chair.

'I fear the vulnerability required in normal love because as a child . . .'

'Oh, don't tell me, please, you were rejected by your mother.'

'No. She loved me but I couldn't express my love for her.'

'No mention of your father, then?'

'No.'

'What was he like?'

He didn't answer. He gave me a fresh unasked-for piece of information instead. 'The consequence of all this is that I could be a sadist.'

'I think you are.'

'Yes, but a particularly extreme type.'

'Oh? How extreme? The bigger the screams the better you like it?'

'The screams don't interest me. The silence does.'

'How so?'

'She thinks I'm a necrophiliac.'

'I get it. You used to be a werewolf but you're all right now.'

'I'm serious.'

I felt the fear return to curdle in my stomach. The drink that had built up my bravado was running out of punch. I didn't really know what was going to happen next, except my brain seemed to be shrinking into a ball of black ice. He was happy to continue.

'That's the diagnosis. I control it, of course. But that's what I am when I invent the world I want to be in.'

'You want to get off by killing me?' I said, fingering my neck, thinking about the disk and the woman's bloody breasts.

'No. I want to get off by you being dead.'

Great. I make a complete hash of things by slipping the chain off the door and now the geek adds insult to injury by playing damned semantics. I began to formulate a plan, a little late perhaps, but a plan nonetheless. I thought if I offered him coffee I could get to the kitchen where the big knives were.

'Coffee?'

'No thanks.'

'Mind if I . . .'

He brought his hand up fast, making me sit still, perching on the edge of the sofa like a sadly exposed hamster eyeing the family cat.

'She told me that death eliminates the risk of rejection, you see, and control over it increases the feeling of supreme power. The killer eliminates his own weakness,

89

exults in his triumph over it. To love death is to love yourself. It's perfect.'

'I think it's overrated myself,' I said. 'Look, could we talk about this some other time?'

'Are you afraid?'

'Afraid? No, why should I be? Christ. We're only talking about screwing dead bodies here, and mine in particular . . .'

'I don't screw dead bodies, I can't think of anything more revolting.'

'Then you've got a hell of a sense of humour, if you don't mind my saying so.'

'You just have to pretend.'

'Lie back and think of Transylvania. Great.'

'Oh, come now. Some women dream of rape, I believe.'

'I don't.'

'Of being overpowered then. Submitting, surrendering.'

'Maybe.'

'Maybe, nothing.'

'David, I don't want to talk about this.'

'Children play, we all have to play, the games change, that's all. If it's just a dream, a play, it's safe.'

'Well, I haven't dreamed you, have I? I haven't dreamed this,' I said, pointing to my neck. His face tensed in annoyance. He'd wanted his smooth reasonableness to overwhelm me but it had failed. There was a matchstick in the corner of his mouth, and two broken ones on his thigh. I looked around for my cigarettes and my Zip lighter.

'You're still seeing the black man,' he said.

'Don't call him that.'

'That's what he is.'

'That's not what you're saying, though.'

'A negro.'

'For Christ's sake.'

'What's his name?'

'He's just an old friend. He was over here on a holiday so he looked me up.'

'What does he do for you?'

'Nothing. Look, David . . .'

'He doesn't know what to do, does he?'

'David. Leave. It's over.'

'Why?'

'I just don't go with married men.'

Well, it was the truth and, in the light of his frank talking, there didn't seem much point in explaining that strangulation wasn't high on my list of indispensable erotic experiences. He'd fixed on to something that he thought I had revealed about myself in that hotel room in New York and nothing was going to shake it. The fact was he had just found himself.

He slipped his hand into his trouser pocket and pulled out something grey and soft. They landed with a flap on the table between us. Surgical gloves.

'Put them on.'

I began to laugh. The gardener on the TV had transplanted the fruit tree. He was talking about mulching now.

'Put them on.'

'No, don't be silly, David. It doesn't work any more. Can't you see?'

He got up and came over, standing so close to the sofa that I had to arch my neck to look up at him. My head felt heavy as I swung it back to look up at him obscuring the light from me. He looked exceptionally tall from down in the dark where I was.

'Put them on.'

'No.'

His hands moved quickly behind my ears and along my jaw, pulling up so I had to stretch my neck an impossible distance if I still planned on sitting down. He hauled me right off the sofa with a rough jerk and crushed his mouth over mine. It was more of a bite than a kiss. I couldn't breathe and I couldn't work out where my legs had gone. I was suffocating. He let me go suddenly and I crashed heavily into the sofa. The alcoholic limescale that furred my mind was clearing fast. I sucked in as much air as I could before leaning past him to take the gloves and slowly stretch the thin latex over my hands. My fingernails looked blackened, my fingers smooth as a cadaver's. He took my hands and felt all around them. I couldn't watch.

'Now touch me,' he said. I opened my eyes to face his groin. His fingers were unbuckling his black belt. So I did what he asked but not what he wanted. I screwed my smooth hand up into a fist and hit him smack between the legs. He jumped backwards with a grunt and collapsed forward in an instant, hands clamped over his testicles, glasses falling from his face on to Richard's springy all-wool Wedgwood-blue carpet. He didn't make another sound, he just rolled from side to side, his eyes closed and his jaws clenched tight.

I got up quickly, stepping over him and grabbing the bottle of wine that I had emptied. I stood over him, my mind sharper now as he pressed his hands down on the floor, pushed himself upright and then bent over slowly and painfully to pick up his spectacles. I put the bottle down.

'For God's sake,' I said, turning away from him. I stood with my back to him, opening a pack of cigarettes and lighting up with trembling fingers. He could have put his hands around my throat easily, struck me across the head, anything. He could have done it then. I waited, tense and afraid, and then turned around quickly.

'You've made a mistake. I don't want any of it,' I said.

'Shit you don't. You want some fucking excitement

just like me. I know. You're as crazy as I am and if we keep it between ourselves who the hell's going to care?'

'Your wife? You wanted to talk about your wife,' I said.

He waited for a slow count of ten and then belted me hard, twice, across the face, and it was my turn to spin backwards. I held my hand to my stinging cheek while blood seeped under my tongue, warm and metallic. His hands shot to my throat and he squeezed, just a little, hard and firm, then he smiled, before lifting his hand and licking away the trickle of red that had fallen on the fair hairs of his hand. He rubbed the index and middle finger of his left hand together like two legs kicking in the air.

'You're nothing until I make you. Nothing at all,' he said.

The sound of the door slamming reverberated around the house. When the tremors stopped I realized that the telephone had been ringing all the while.

'Mrs Powers?'

'Yes?'

'Robert Falk. Not an inopportune time, I hope?'

I shrank back from the sight of my gloved hand covering the mouthpiece. I put the receiver down with a clatter on the table and shredded them from my hands. I picked up the phone again, conscious of the fine powder covering my fingers, now dusting the hard black plastic of the handset. My mouth felt as if it were pumped with Novocaine.

'No. Great. Robert. How are you? Did you find anything?' I mumbled.

'Fine, Georgina. And no. There doesn't appear to be a missing person answering this lady's description.'

'Oh.'

'For what it's worth, I think the program's a fake.'

I desperately wanted to sit down. My head was beginning to ache and swim.

'It's not a real snuff?' I said.

'No, I don't think so. Had a word with Obscene Publications and they say the only snuff-like sequences they've ever seen have either been out and out shams or horrible mixes of special effects and actual documentary footage of Third World torture.'

'No traceable victims?'

'Put it this way, no one's ever been charged with a snuff movie murder, not to my knowledge, anyway.'

'Oh,' I said, and we were both silent until he said, 'There is one thing, Georgina . . . are you still there?'

'Yes.' Barely.

'Unless you're one for sports, you wouldn't notice, but the man's actions are not dissimilar to, well . . . a tennis player's. You look at it again. Looks like someone's having you on.'

CHAPTER NINE

Warren had left a number for me to call just in case I needed to get in touch. It had been three weeks since he'd given it to me and I hadn't used it once. I dialled and the Savoy replied. Warren answered a couple of minutes later.

'Comfortable?' I said.

'Not bad.'

'The Savoy, eh? You didn't say.'

'You didn't ask. You all right?'

'Yeah, why?'

'Your voice sounds funny.'

'I've had a visitor. Warren, I want to show you something. I need you here.'

'Need me? Now?'

'Now.'

He said it was a bit awkward for him to come right away on account of the fact that it was late, and he had company. I swore and put the phone down as Richard came in through the door. He looked at me, and then looked hard again, his hand on my chin.

'Oh bloody hell,' he said.

'You should have seen the other guy,' I replied.

He pushed past me, angry about more than one thing but mostly, he was angry at me. Or at least, that's what I thought at the time.

'You let this bloke walk in here and knock you about?'

he roared, clanging pots out of his way and hauling out the cafetière from its hiding place. 'Get me a drink. God, woman. A brandy. Get me a brandy.'

I scurried to the front room for the bottle and a bulbous glass to pour it in, while Richard was aggressively spooning ground Algerian into the chrome and glass jug. I put the glass and the bottle on the table and told him I was off to bed. Richard spun round and roared again like a bull whose nose ring was too tight. 'You're going nowhere. Sit down and shut up.'

'Now look . . .' I said, reckoning that I'd had about enough for one night.

'Look nothing. I don't like your friends, Georgina. I don't like them coming in here and doing what the hell they like. They're low life. Where's your respect for yourself? For me? Your parents? Christ knows what they think next door.'

I think it was the mention of my parents, or maybe of the people next door, that twanged my stretched-out patience back like a whiplash. It contracted at speed to a small, hard, heavy, black coal that burned so much I had to heft it at someone. I put my hand out and made do with the smooth, round brandy glass instead. It skimmed past Richard's ear like a miniature heat-seeking missile directly towards the pole of woks and pots. It struck one of the larger heavy-based pans hard, and rained shiny, vicious splinters all over the double oven. I'd picked up the bottle of brandy too, but Richard made it over in time to wrench it from my hand. He grabbed me by the shoulders and shook me. I screamed and kicked his leg, his bad leg. He staggered back on to the table, knocking the bottle over, and rolled over on to a chair.

'You bitch. You fucking bitch,' he said, rubbing his shin and groaning as I hurried down the hall to my room.

I took off my clothes as if they were on fire and flung them into a corner. I stalked from one end of the room to another before sitting down at the dressing table to contemplate me, and my face. There was just a little bit of blood under my nose and at the side of my mouth. The bruises still ringed my neck but my eyes were all right, a little bleary from drink, a little firm with temper, but all right. Tomorrow, I decided, I'd start packing. To hell with them. To hell with them all. I was going home to mother.

The door bell rang about three-quarters of an hour later. Richard answered it and straight away, voices were raised.

'What the hell's going on?' I said, opening my bedroom door and yelling down the hall. Warren stood half in the door, toe to toe with Richard, who was still fully dressed and reeking of brandy. Warren took a look at me hurrying towards them and turned to Richard, his face taut and serious.

'What's going on?' he said.

'You tell me,' Richard replied, pushing his chest forward.

Warren shoved it back hard with the palm of his hand, and asked me. 'What's happened, George?'

'I thought you were spoken for tonight?' I said.

Warren smiled and, forgetting about Richard, held out both hands. 'Hey, I can pop out for five minutes, carn' I?'

I didn't have time to answer because Richard swung his fist at an astonished Warren and caught him firmly on the jaw. I grabbed Richard's arm as he prepared to swing again. Warren recovered quickly and ducked, fists up to defend himself.

Richard began to shout. 'You bastard. One a night not enough for you? You black bastard.'

I hung on to his arm and wrestled him inside the hallway where he continued to curse Warren over my head. I kicked the door shut in Warren's face.

'What the hell do you think you're doing?' I shrieked and Richard yelled right back.

'I'm glad I punched the bastard. He roughs you up, fucks off with my girl, and comes over here for seconds. Open that blasted door.'

'Are you serious?'

'Open it or . . .'

'I asked Warren to come over here to help me with that story. Warren didn't do this. Warren isn't involved in any of this.'

Richard kicked the door. 'He still fucked off with my girl.'

'Diane?'

'Who do you think?'

I pulled Richard back and leaned my back against the door. Then I pointed down the hall and Richard moved back a couple of steps while I crouched down and cautiously lifted up the flap of the letter box.

'Warren?'

'Yeah.'

'Piss off.'

It's what kitchen tables are for: two glasses, two pairs of elbows and a bottle of brandy. Richard had apologized, I had apologized, and Warren was on his way back to his plush cocoon in the Strand and the sleepy arms of Diane Shine.

'What else was I s'posed to think?' said Richard, drunker now that I was sobering up.

'Well, it's not Warren.'

'Bastard.'

'You called him a black bastard.'

'He fucking is.'

'Diane's black, blacker than Warren.'

'She's gorgeous. The bitch.'

'OK. What happened?'

98

Richard began at the end. He told me how Warren had turned up at some party Diane and he were at. It didn't occur to him that she must have invited him. Warren was hardly in a position to move in on a social life that involved media-rich house parties.

'How do you know they went together?'

Richard raised his heavy head and stared me down like a tolerant bloodhound.

'No see you laters?' I said.

'No.'

'How come she left with him?'

'He said, "You coming?" and she left, I suppose.'

'She comes with you but leaves with him. Oh, bad manners.'

'More than that, George.'

Richard's sodden, heavy-lidded eyes stared glumly over his glass. He grasped the neck of the bottle and reached over to pour me a generous measure of brandy. 'Women. Bloody hell,' he said. 'You make rules, they find a way to break 'em for you.'

'Now hang on . . .' I said.

'Hang on, nothing. Can't trust 'em. Nope. Can't trust 'em.'

'Oh, shut up. You got dumped. End of story.'

'Thanks.'

I looked hard at Richard's bowed head. 'How close?'

'Closey close. We were an item.'

'Item, as in one?'

Richard nodded miserably and burbled into his brandy. 'I don't know. She's so beautiful, George, and funny and sweet . . .'

'But not loyal.'

'No, not loyal.'

He shook his head and I gripped mine. Things had changed since Diane and I had had our little chat in the bar at IPEX. A couple of weeks ago, Diane Shine was rubbing her knees together at the thought of him. She'd worked fast and she'd got him. He must have been a hell of a disappointment for her to quit so soon. Apart from anything else, he could make or break her career at *Technology Week*. That alone would have been worth faking it for a month at least. Unless, of course, she had something better in mind.

'So what rule did she make you break then?' I said.

'You know. Never go out with people you work with.'

'She made you. You didn't want to, of course.'

'Huh?'

'No others, I suppose?'

'What?'

'Rules.'

'She's a hard woman to refuse, George.'

'Oh, stop jerking me about. What did you tell her?'

'You what?' he said.

I wanted to grab Richard by the wilted lapels of his damp polo shirt and yank him across the table. The irritation in my voice shocked him into paying more attention. His rumpled face wobbled a little and his red-rimmed, clueless eyes blinked a couple of times as if someone was shining a light at them in the darkness beneath heavy blankets.

'Richard,' I said. 'Did you tell her about my story?'

He leaned on to his elbows and covered his eyes.

'Did she ask you about it?'

'I suppose so. Yes. I suppose so,' he said, his hands over his face.

'Well, thank you. Thank you very much,' I replied and slung what was left of my brandy into the sink.

I went to my room and picked up my extension. Warren took a while to answer the phone.

'That you?' he said.

'She still there?'

'Yeah.'

'She awake?'

'Nah.'

'Wake her.'

'C'mon, George.'

'Wake her.'

Diane's dry voice answered after about thirty seconds. 'Hello?'

'Warren tell you what you wanted to know?'

'What?'

'Or have you got to work a bit harder?'

'Now look . . .'

'You look. This is my story. Understand?'

'No law says it has to be.'

'No, but let's just say your cover is blown.'

'Couldn't this wait until Monday morning?'

'No. You'll be too busy.'

'How come?'

'How does six months' worth of product surveys grab you?'

'We'll see about that,' she said. 'Oh and by the way . . .'

'Yes?'

'Warren here sends his love.'

I clicked the receiver into its cradle and stared at the box on my desk. She had it all.

The next morning I was up late, but before Richard, and after two large pots of tea and a brunch of toast and cheese, I didn't feel too bad. My head ached a little and my mouth was sore, but I didn't feel sick. I couldn't stand that, the sour nausea of a hangover was worse than going without, almost. I had a shower and went back to my room to look for a bikini or a swimsuit that might do. It was eleven o'clock in the morning and the sun was already high in the sky, burning down on the garden of yellowing grass and daisies that led down to the still water of the canal behind the house. The old lady who lived in the basement flat had the garden but Richard had built a pink and grey sun trap for himself above. It was a little piece of the Mediterranean that served his kitchen with pungent green and silver herbs, and delighted his eye with scarlet geraniums in terracotta pots. I was out in the sunshine unfolding a striped canvas lounger when the front door bell rang. It was my old friend, Warren.

'Had breakfast?' I enquired.

'Can I come in?' he replied.

I told him Richard was in his room and left him at the door while I strolled back to my drink and the lounger.

He followed, watching me settle back and relax. 'Your mouth don't look too bad. He do it? David?' he said, looking down at me.

'You're in my sun,' I replied.

He stepped to one side and the bright heat radiated on to my pill-white skin. I closed my eyes behind my dark glasses. I wasn't going to tell him that I was working, working at staying alive.

'What you drinking?' he said.

I dropped an arm over the side and rattled the ice in the glass tucked just under the seat.

'Juice.'

'Oh.'

'Surprised?'

'Just thirsty.'

'Help yourself.'

He didn't. I opened my eyes behind the glasses. He stood leaning back, with his hands on the low wall that stretched around the little yard, his back to the grey council flats and the blue sky beyond. He wore a baggy white pure cotton T-shirt that trembled a little in the light breeze, sucking in and out over his lean chest and stomach. The sound of traffic ebbed and flowed from the road by the park mixed with a little birdsong from the eaves above us and the garden below. I took a sip from my drink and lay back again.

'You used to be discreet, Warren. What happened?'

'So I slept with 'er. So what?'

'To laugh in Richard's face?'

'She chose. She don't belong to no one.'

I hated him for saying the right thing. I should have said it to Richard last night. I should have told him that what was really bugging him was Warren, that most of all, he hadn't wanted to lose to him. David Jones felt the same way. I couldn't blame them; after all, I knew what it was like.

'So what did you tell her?'

He didn't answer. He seemed to find the scrubby lawn below more interesting.

'Did she get the inside track from you on the story? Must have done. You would have told her, wouldn't you? You wouldn't have just screwed her and not come across, would you? Well, how can you blame her? A story like this could give her an in with the nationals. A girl can't pass up an opportunity like that, can she? Or did you tell her you were rich? Yes, that would have worked. It can't have all gone. No . . . can't have, not with a suite in the Savoy. My, my . . . that must have impressed her. The job wouldn't have done. I mean, security guard doesn't cut it, does it? Must still have some left, what with all the gear and the flash hotel.'

He kept his eyes looking down until he was sure that I had finished. Then he looked up at the house, taking in the detail, brick by brick. Time passed and, though the harsh sun made me want to close my eyes, I watched him and waited until he had to speak.

'You wouldn't think she wanted me for myself then?' he said, staring at the windows now as if fascinated by the drapes. It was a gift and if he thought I wouldn't take it, he was wrong.

'Not if she knew what I knew, she wouldn't.'

I saw his fingers whiten as he clenched the top of the low wall and chewed his lower lip. I'd got to him this time. For a moment, I felt exultant, so puffed with pleasure that my heart could have popped out on the patio and danced a disgusting jig of delight. It didn't last. My hate was so insubstantial that regret pushed it aside immediately with all its heavy baggage in tow.

'I'm sorry,' I said.

'Yeah?'

'I am.'

'You don't forgive, do you?'

'I do . . . sometimes.'

'The fuck you do.'

I clicked the back of the lounger so it lay completely flat, turned over on to my stomach and flicked the clasp of my top apart. He didn't leave. He stood there for a quarter of an hour while I baked, my head resting heavily on my oily arms, my eyes shut tight. Then I heard his footsteps on the flagstones, heard him stop and his knees click as he crouched down. My skin twitched as his cool hand touched the warm skin on my back. The fine brown hairs on my arms prickled and my nipples hardened like hazelnuts.

'You'll burn,' he said.

I straightened up on my elbows to turn and look at him. He wasn't David, but David had said that.

'I want to,' I said.

'Why?'

'My skin's too pale.'

'You want to tan, take it easy.'

'Thanks for the advice. Now, what does she know, Warren?'

He sighed and rested back on his heels. 'She told me she knew about the game.'

'And?'

104

'She wanted to know what I'd told you. I told her that I'd played it.'

'And?'

'Well, the details got to us a little, tell you the truth.'

I had to laugh. Warren waited a couple of moments and when he was sure that I really found it funny, he joined in. The giggling left me aching down my sides. I pointed my finger over my shoulder for Warren to snap the clasp of my top shut so that I could decently rise from the lounger.

'Come on,' I said, 'I want to show you something.'

'Please God,' he replied and I hit him on the leg.

He watched Julie Wentworth's banana song over my prawn-pink shoulder without changing the rhythm of his breathing. Watching it with him made me hold my breath. I didn't say anything about it while I loaded the second.

'I don't know for sure about the first one,' he said, tapping the screen. 'But this one with 'im's a fake.'

'This one? Are you sure?'

'Yeah . . . yeah, I'm sure.' He looked at me. 'All right?' he said.

'No. How do you know it's a fake?' I said.

He tapped the dying woman's bloody breasts. 'Well, I've seen 'er before.'

'Where?'

'Level ten. Big deal in Pornoland. Do it, watch it but if you get snuffed you lose the game. Whoever's playing him is winning and whoever picked her, is losing. She was a main character.'

'You recognize him, of course. Come on. You said you did. You saw him outside the pub, said he was in the game.'

No reply.

'Warren?'

'Yeah. I did.'

I peered at the screen and thought what Robert Falk had said. Tennis. David played tennis. His arms were lightly tanned. Maybe Falk was right.

'Don't look at her, Warren. Sit down. Look at him. What does it look like he's doing?'

Warren started the whole thing again, leaning back so that the chair rocked a little on its two back legs. His brown arms were folded across his chest and his face creased in a frown. David came towards him like a jerky villain from an old home movie.

'Squash? Tennis?' he volunteered at the end.

I sat down on the edge of the bed, wiping my hand over my face. Robert Falk was right. The program was a nasty little fake just like the other one she'd given me, and the one Warren had won in Las Vegas. There had to be more, all destined for the game, little sequences for the players to watch when they made the right, or the wrong, move. So, David hadn't killed anyone, yet.

'Tennis. I don't know why I didn't see it before.'

He hesitated before he said, 'Maybe you know something I don't.'

I lay back, my hands over my eyes. They had started to throb a little and the skin on my neck felt tight. The disks might be fake but Warren was right, I had had a taste of what was real.

'You all right?' Warren said.

'Yes.'

'You let him hurt you?'

'I didn't let him.'

I was trying not to cry but a hot drip slid from my eye past my ear and into my hair. I kept my hands over my face and hoped he wouldn't notice the thickening of my voice.

'It could have been me, you know,' I said.

'He tried to kill you?'

'I'm not sure.'

'He wants to make you think about it.'

I didn't answer. I had to tell somebody but the shame of someone else knowing was going to be worse than the shame of knowing myself. I had to tell Warren I'd been a fool and I didn't want to. I kept my eyes closed, my lips pressed together to stop any sobs that might have shuddered out of me. The bed gave slightly as Warren sat down on the edge. I could smell my hot, oiled skin and a breath of light cologne from his. It was quiet in the room, and still, until I felt his cool, brown fingers creeping round my neck.

I think I shouted as my hands scraped desperately at his. He shook me so the yells drowned in my throat. When I realized that I could still scream and breathe the panic receded a fraction and my eyes blinked at his, caught in an astonished expression of horror. His hands gripped my struggling shoulders and though I could see his mouth moving, I couldn't hear. He drew me to him, holding me hard against his chest, muttering through my hair and stroking his hands over my back until the tension, coiling like an eel inside, loosened to nothing. I put my arms around his waist and held him tight. I didn't cry until he said, 'Oh, Georgina.'

Oh, Georgina, what a fool you've been. What a fool. Oh, hear me. Warren help me. Let not the man who is beast or who thinks he is God come near me. Through the sobs and broken sentences, Warren held me like a baby and kissed my head.

'Warren . . .'

'Don't have to say anything,' he said.

We lay for a while side by side staring at the ceiling.

'You know how much I love you?' he said.

'Enough to tell Diane?'

'I told Diane.'

There was movement in the kitchen and Warren made

me brush my hair, wipe my eyes and go to see if I could pre-empt any trouble. Richard was half leaning, half hanging against a cupboard. He had the look of a man who had spent the night being regurgitated by an anaconda to whom he had just lost the fight of his life. Steam from a boiling kettle puffed energetically around him like the sulphurous fumes of some small hell. I didn't laugh; I'd been where Richard was too many times not to know how much it can hurt.

'Warren's here, in my room. We're trying to get into that game. No problem, I hope?' I said.

Eyes tightly shut, Richard shook his head with care. I made three cups of coffee and opened up a pack of paracetamol for him. As I walked back to the bedroom, I heard him running hard for the bathroom.

Warren watched me put the cups on the dressing table.

'You've got real skinny,' he said.

'No tits, no ass, but don't you love the moustache?'

'If you had one, I'd love it. How about a holiday?'

'With you?'

'With me. Anywhere you want.'

'Give me the number of the game, Warren, and I'll think about it.'

'You know your trouble, babe?'

'What's that?'

'You're too fucking romantic.'

CHAPTER TEN

Late Monday morning after I had been to the hairdresser
for a short back and sides and a ferocious bleach,
Richard rang to say that Diane wasn't at work. I was
busy plugging the Pony machine into the modem that
usually served my PC. I had my head under the desk and
the phone on hands-free.

'She's not at home either,' he said.

'So be a good dog and howl.'

'I'm worried.'

'Have you spoken to her since Friday?'

'Yes. Saturday night. We talked, you know . . .'

'And?'

'She said she had a lead on the game story.'

'My story . . .'

'. . . and was going to follow it up. She said she'd be in
Monday morning.'

'Warren was with me, Richard.'

'I know.'

'What was the lead?' I said.

'She said she had a name.'

'Uh huh. She say what it was?'

'No.'

I rang the Savoy.

'Mr Graham has checked out.'

'Are you sure?'

'This morning, madam.'

I put the receiver down slowly. She'd gone and he'd gone. The happy couple had skipped. She had been able to move fast thanks to Richard and Warren's talking-talking-talking happy talk. Anger was my first response. I should have known better than to trust him. The man was an opportunist, a dipper. I should never have let him know me. He wasn't trying to help me, he was helping himself, always helping himself. I just couldn't make him out. On Sunday, we'd had a picnic in the park. We'd been together, laughing and fooling around. I'd been happy with him, I was starting to trust him.

I looked at the machine. He'd given me the number, but he hadn't done anything else. He could have set up the kit and shown me how to play the game. Maybe, he was just trying to slow me up so that Diane could get a head start. He knew I'd be trying to kickstart the communications link all by myself with the help of a brain-shredding manual as thick as a telephone directory, and with no guarantee that the number he'd given me was going to get me past the starting blocks. He'd kept me occupied over the weekend while, I stake my life on it, she was beavering away in the office. He'd wanted me to be tied up for a while. So be it, but why make such a party of it? That was what hurt.

I tinkered and fiddled for an hour and more, until the screen gave me the go and I tapped in the number. It rang four times, clicked, and a little square appeared with the thickly lettered legend – Pornoland – and terse instructions informing me that payment was strictly by credit card. It hadn't all been lies, then. I had to log on with my card number, just as Warren had told me. The fee was a one-off payment for membership followed by an hourly on-line fee. It was steep, but I comforted myself with the notion that at least it was tax-deductible. I logged on and pressed the keyboard so that I could dump the screen picture on my printer. I needed some proof, and quickly, because if Diane Shine had her little chat with David, my bet was there would be a blank screen for everyone for a while.

The word 'accepted' appeared shortly after I tapped my number in. I was informed that Pornoland was a sophisticated adult role-playing adventure game which nevertheless required some arcade skill. The aim in each of the worlds was to control territory, markets and people in order to make a profit. The one who made the most money, but not necessarily the one who captured the largest territory, won. To do this it would be necessary to generate revenue, co-operate with and intimidate others, and, naturally enough, survive. Since it was a multi-user game, once I had selected a character, I would be pitted against others, some of whom had been playing for some time and would already be established.

It took some time to get down the line, but what I got in the end was a stroboscopic burst of three-dimensional vector graphics – a wonder of trigonometry and matrix algebra in full motion. It was like flying at speed through a line drawing of Miami at night. Every now and then the screen would bank past a window and there would be a still shot of a woman pouting, or stripping or lying back or on her knees for someone. A child would lick a lollipop or a dog would run tail up down an alley full of dustbins. There would be a policeman on the corner or a hearse, or an ambulance turning into a street, lights flashing blue, and glimmering in the distance was a casino, lit up like a shrine.

The screen filled with dollar bills which grew to obliterate everything and suddenly sank in the middle as if you, the flier, had fallen on to a soft pillow of cash. All was dark and the logo of Pornoland glowed like gold.

A door opened in the dark green to a bright, comic-book office where a filing cabinet lay open in the corner. Across the screen was a list of the highest scorers to date and the biggest losers. I looked for Warren's name. There was Sven and Lars, Bambino and Pussy, Chan and Plumber – the top six were in credit but their pseudonyms told me nothing. Warren was no Sven and no Bambino. I glanced at the losers' list and there, right at the bottom, was the name Cabbie by the awful score of minus £250,000. It had to be him. That's what he used to be, a cabbie. But he never said he had lost. He said he had won me, and that he had got out into the operating system. I didn't understand what it could mean, but there wasn't time to work anything out. I had to select my character from the greyish photos that were popping up from the cabinet and were lining up in a grid of stills like a contact sheet.

There was no picture of me. That meant I couldn't be a player. That's what Warren had said. I was an option. If someone won, as Warren had done, my head, and whoever it was had donated the better-endowed body, came out to perform for a ten-second ogle. There was no shot of Julie Jones, which meant that she wasn't available as an identity for players to assume either. Maybe she was a secondary character like the composite of me, for those who won the right to see a bad blow job. There had to be some booby prizes, I suppose.

The passport-sized pictures flicked through the screen and though Warren had warned me that he'd recognized David from Pornoland, it was still a shock to see his photo there. The lettering beneath the small serious portrait made me sit back in surprise too. It explained why Warren had been reluctant to help me find it. The words 'Cabbie (now off-line)' glowed in green. My mouth went dry. Warren had chosen David as his alter ego. He knew everything there was to know about him, and still picked him. It was hard to take. I chewed my lip and blinked back the tears as I pointed the screen cursor at the photo, clicked and got a summary of the character's abilities.

No surprises. This one was a computer specialist who scored high on IQ, high on sexual appetite and average on physical ability. He had a reasonable criminality rating, high intelligence, and a high mental disorder score. Cautious but no coward, he had stores of aggressive potential. His sexual equipment was normal. It was David all right. If he'd written it, there would be no reason for the facts to be wrong. He hadn't boosted his physical ability as any other man would have. Captain Weird must like himself just as he was. What had Warren seen in him? Frankly, what had I? I scanned the picture for the woman, the one Cabbie had slashed. She was there all right and underneath her picture was written 'Lulu', but the screen scrolled on and I didn't have time to go back and check how much she had lost. Death must cost a fortune.

Cabbie 'off-line' meant Warren wasn't playing. In fact, no one was on-line at all. I reckoned that players in the UK would be playing at night, to take advantage of the cheaper rates after work. Anyone tuning in from abroad would have to take account of the time differences. The screen warned me that since no one else was on-line, I'd be playing the computer and that I could only play it at the lower levels. I scanned the list, making sure to print out what I saw. Eventually, I settled for a good-looking Japanese chap, three squares from the right, three lines down. He was a wrestler, physically agile, with an above-average IQ. He was not a coward and had some business acumen. His sexual appetite was low to average, his criminality high and mental disorder level minuscule. He was also much better hung than your average bear.

The computer asked for my codename. I tapped in the name 'Bruce' and waited. The photo shrank into a corner and a little yellow sprite, with straight shiny black hair, chunky legs and a big bulge in his groin, popped out and walked stiffly into a bar called Dicky's. So far, so puerile. A little square of text told me that there was a peep show in progress behind a door in the far corner. Bruce had to get to it without having to buy a round, i.e. parting with money. Now I understood why you could only play the computer at the lower levels. A good games player would second guess the machine and break the bank. Since there were no real live humans to play against, the only obstacles were a beckoning woman and a large-muscled moustachioed creature, with what appeared to be a pit bull terrier. Up in the corner, the odds against defeating the characters flashed. I could place bets in real money which would add to my score if I won. If I lost, my credit card would be in full flex.

The woman, I noticed, was high risk on the sexual front but Bruce's profile told me that he wasn't that susceptible. She also had a plate of steak and chips on the table beside her. Though Bruce was agile, Mr Moustache did have a dog. I selected the woman and as Bruce drew closer I was given a short close-up of her breasts. The screen showed a pair of real breasts of Hindenberg proportions, under an acre of diaphanous material. Bruce's options were to satisfy the lady and get her to take him to the door or wrestle her for her dinner. Bruce chose to play for the dinner and not pay for the pneumatic lady. He wrestled to victory unmoved by her gameplan of grabbing at his genitals. He refused sex with the muscleman and refused to buy him a drink. Incensed, the man set his ferocious dog on him. Quick-thinking Bruce threw the steak over the bar, distracted man and beast and ran past them to the mystery door. He won me one hundred for doing that, and he and I were just looking in on the peep show when the screen went blank. My printer stopped. I lifted the long sheet of paper. All I had was a few shots that wouldn't make a magistrate blush. Diane Shine must have made contact and David had wisely pulled the plug.

I sat back in the chair, my shoulder blades still a little tender from the sun. I looked at the printout, then at the Pony, my mind very much on Warren. How far up the greasy pole had Warren got to make his boy David kill Lulu and how come he had picked that option for his man, anyway? It upset me to think of him pressing the buttons. I hoped that he had had no option, that he had to do it because there was no other way he could go. It was only a game but that was no comfort.

There was one question that I wanted answered. If he'd picked the right option, how come he lost £250,000? He had said that he was winning. She was losing. I couldn't see it being any other way.

Dread was getting in the way of my thinking. Pornoland, as the machine had warned, was just like real life and I could see it had unfolded around me without the aid of electronics. David was real for me. He and I had played an elaborate game of fantasy but there were real consequences and I'd realized too late how dangerous it could be. It meant abusing his wife, working me over, hemming me in, until there would be only one place for me to go for him to win. Out. Right out. Just like Lulu.

I had no gameplan of my own, that was the problem, and outside the machine you couldn't just press a button and switch everything off. I realized with dismay how real a game was being played and the computer was just a way of keeping score.

Lying next to the Pony were the disks Julie Jones had given me, and the one Warren had brought from Las Vegas. I had to look at them all again. The disks were the same size – 3.5 inches – and without thinking I slotted one of Julie's into the Pony's drive. Before I hit the keyboard to run the program, I'd flicked the thing out again. I stared at it and mentally kicked myself. It wasn't going to run. That metaphorical lightbulb flashed over my head. Of course it wouldn't. It couldn't. It had run on the PC in the office and on my PC here. It was IBM PC-compatible, not Pony-compatible.

The IBM PC is the most common personal computer in the world. It's the pit pony of business, a standard. The Pony is not, it's a games machine, a whizzy bronco, which is why it had stayed in a cardboard box in my room for so long. Computers are not my idea of fun. To me, they're as much fun as typewriters. To Warren, they're as much fun as you can have without the aid of a Wet and Wild. My idea of fun is getting drunk while watching a gardening programme.

I laughed out loud. Diane didn't have it all, after all. She had nothing at all, and I wasn't a selectable option now, I had just become a primary player.

I picked up the phone and dialled Richard at *Technology Week*. He sounded weary.

'Richard? What's on her desk?'

'Oh, come and look for your frigging self,' he said and cut me off.

Richard had been under pressure. His girl had betrayed him and done a bunk with a guy who had half busted his leg. He'd spent one half of the weekend in a stupor and the other prostrate with pain. To cap it all, Essex had eclipsed Middlesex in an eight-wicket victory inside two days to clinch the County Championship. I wished I had his worries.

It was gone lunchtime and the office was nearly empty when I hurried in. If the journalists weren't at press conferences, press day wasn't imminent enough for anyone to rush back to work. I nodded to Richard, who was taking the lid off a take-away from the local salad bar. He nodded back, staring for a moment at my hair as he did so. This morning it had been long and dark, now it was short and white-blonde like ripples in an ancient marble head. I was happy with the look, especially since my pink skin was peeling a little and shading to brown. The hardest thing was finding something in my wardrobe that wasn't black. I settled for a blue denim shift and a red sailor's kerchief to knot round my neck. If David ever got to see the new me, he wasn't going to want it. I wasn't his living doll any more.

Diane's desk was neat and organized. Mine was not. I see disorganization as a fundamental key to security. It means no one knows where to look. Diane's desk was laid out like a map. Her contact book had gone, but her desk diary, spare notebooks, pens and a soppy crumpled note from my landlord furnished a tidy top drawer. I looked in the diary; there were no appointments for today. The red in-tray on her desk contained four neatly stacked plastic folders of releases relating to stories she was working on. The green tray underneath was solid with paper. I lifted much of it out. It was the exhibitors' list for IPEX.

My finger scanned the names and addresses to the end. It was clear that one was missing. The one where Virtech should have been. That meant she had noted the address, telephone and fax number, and David's name as managing director.

I pulled more paper from the tray, sheaf after sheaf of names and addresses of all those who had attended IPEX, the visitors' list. What a treasure. Warren had suggested that I get the list, and here it was, on Diane's desk. I shook my head. I'd asked her to get all this for me, and that's when her little nose wrinkled with the whiff of a story. Richard had laid the trail that had set her tracking me for a by-line. She'd been on to my story for a while. I went through the visitors' list again. The page where Julie Jones might have been was missing too. Tiny palpitations began in my chest. Julie Jones could have, must have, been there. She could have seen us meet.

I picked up the telephone and dialled internal. Max Winters came on-line.

'Max, sorry to trouble you . . .'

'Working on the story, are we?' he said.

I looked across the room at his ginger cat head behind his terminal. His lips pulled softly on a small cigar and he smiled over at me. It was as affable as a grin on a Great White.

'Yes. Was Diane in on Saturday?'

'First thing.'

'Did she make any calls?'

'I think so.'

'Thanks.'

I'd spent Saturday sunbathing. Warren had left and come back to take me to a movie and some late supper. He was such a natural liar. Breathtaking. They deserved each other. I flicked again through the folders in the red tray until my eye rested on one containing a release from Babylon Software Ltd. It was a company specializing in games programs. I picked it up and in the middle of the first page, the name 'Julie Jones, top games designer' was highlighted in acid yellow. The press release was an announcement of a new game from Babylon – Voyage to the Zigurrat. Julie Jones knew her way around a computer like an ant carrying a dead thing knew its way home.

Attached to the back of the release with a steel paperclip was a note bearing the words 'Check MT Industries, & Holdings' in Diane's handwriting. I didn't recognize the name so I went to the bank of grey steel filing cabinets that lined the far wall of the office by the photocopiers. I looked under 'M', 'J' and under 'B'. There was a potted biography and picture of Julie Jones under 'J', and Babylon's company résumé under 'B'. There was nothing for MT Industries under 'M'.

Babylon Software was one of the most innovative

producers of adventure games in the country. I'd heard of it but that was all. Computer games weren't covered much in the pages of *Technology Week*. The paper left that to the hot little consumer magazines that packed the high street bookstalls. The fact was that Julie Jones was no mere housewife. She had created some of the most popular computer games around. She and her husband might be a team, but she was the gamesmaster.

Diane was right on her tail. She'd found out what JJ 1000 was, and to where it led. All she had to do was look at what she had in these files, make some connections and she was off and running – with Warren. She was doing well but I reckoned I still had an edge. I had played the game, I had the disks and I could write the story, now. Even though Julie had pulled the plug, I had enough. My mind said to go for it, but my pride said wait. A news story was one thing, and Mrs Jones quite another. I wanted to know what she had been setting me up for. It was time to give her a call.

'Julie?'

'Yes. Georgina.' That soft Scots voice rolled down the line without even asking who I was. She didn't have to ask, I bet she felt she had created me.

'I've got a little query.'

'Oh yes?'

'The disks you gave me.'

'Uh huh.'

'They were compatible with my PC, not a Pony on which I know this game runs. Did you take the trouble to do that, put the sequences on a disk that I could use?'

'I did,' she said.

'Maybe we should have a little chat, then.'

'Yes,' she said. 'How about my place?'

'Where's that?'

'The number you just dialled comes into Virtech when I'm not at home.'

I put the phone down fast. What a game she had played. The wife had had her revenge. The mistress had been scared, exposed and made to look foolish.

I could have strangled myself and made David's day. Those disks had lain there on my desk for weeks, and I hadn't seen the difference. Disks from a Pony will not run on a PC: their disk capacities are different and, even if they fit, the operating system on the PC would reach edge city trying to fathom what the hell they were all about.

I called over the cable-strewn office to Richard, who was opening his carton of fruit salad. The man appeared to be trying to lose some weight. Maybe Diane's beauty had made him self-conscious. He had a moody look on his face.

'Can I borrow your car?'

Richard looked back down at his fruit salad and pretended he hadn't heard correctly. I don't know why a man like him drove a Scirocco anyway. To my mind it was a fast car for the ladies, a Volkswagen with some poke.

'Can you drive, then?' he asked, spooning some kiwi fruit and pineapple into his mouth.

''Course I can.'

'Never seen you.'

'I can drive, just can't see the point in London.'

''Course not. You can't drink and drive, can you?'

'Oh, that's a good one,' I said, getting up and walking over.

'What's with the new look?' he said, digging around for a disintegrated strawberry.

'My boyfriend, you know, the one you haven't met but would like to turn into guacamole. He likes long, dark hair.'

'So do I.'

'Good. So what about the car? I have to get up the

M11 to talk to someone about this story. Might as well walk as go via King's Cross.'

'Mmm.'

'Has Diane phoned in?'

'No. Did you find anything?'

'Enough to tell me that the game is no more.'

'Tipped our hand, did she?'

'Yes, but I've got something. I was playing when the game went down. You'll have your story.'

'Good. So how was it for you?'

'I won one hundred, got to see some big breasts and peep at a nice lady *in flagrante*.'

He grunted again and pressed his mouth down on the juicy dessert like a man eating lemons. Richard was not in news editor mode. He was in jilted, unlovable, pain in the ass mode. The only reason I didn't up-end the fruit carton in his miserable face was that he hadn't handed over the keys to his car yet. He was wise to be cautious. I hadn't driven a car in ten years.

'I've got disks with some faces on, Richard. Faces of persons well known in our business. They were into the game. I need to talk to one of them today. Diane won't get anything, I'm telling you.'

Richard leaned back, thrust his hand into his pocket and dragged out his keys.

'So much as one scratch. I mean it,' he said.

CHAPTER ELEVEN

It took hours. I had to get home, pick up the car, and practise clutch and gear changes while negotiating the gridlock traffic in the East End. I took in the leafier side of high-rise Hackney and made it across the marshes and motorways to comfortable Woodford, gateway to Essex, haven of highwaymen, blaggers, fences and those gold-throated *nouveaux riches* who'd made their money in market stalls and office cleaning. By the time I got to that uncongested artery that is the M11, the evening rush hour was building up fast behind me.

I travelled for an hour past the flat fields and superstores of Hertfordshire into Cambridgeshire, turning off into a mini Science Park in which all the buildings appeared to have been constructed by a small child out of coloured shapes of styrofoam. Virtech Ltd was no different from the rest, except that it was a flatter, squarer waffle brick. I parked in the courtesy car-park and wandered up a shrub-lined flagstone path towards the security doors. It was gone six o'clock, the doors were locked and no one was in Reception. I pressed the buzzer and peered through the thick brown-tinted glass. Five minutes later, Julie Jones opened the door.

'Och, you must be desperate. He won't like that,' she said, leading me down a corridor to a windowless conference room at the end.

'You mean the hair?'

'Everything. He wants you dead good-looking, remember?' she said, opening the door. She had known all along. I thought that I would be embarrassed, but I wasn't. When I thought she didn't know, I had been embarrassed, every time we met. It was different now; she wasn't a victim any more, she was an adversary. We sat opposite each other across the shine of a walnut conference table like two nations in a cold war.

'Anyone else been here?' I said.

'Your friend, Warren, and a young hustler called Diane Shine. Rather stole your thunder.'

'What did you tell her?'

'Nothing at all.'

'OK. So tell me. Why did you set me up?'

'With the digitized video?' she replied. 'He wanted me to.'

'Did you enjoy it?' I said, trying to figure out if I believed her.

'David's a mirror. He shows you what you want. Then he gives it to you. You just have to reciprocate a little.'

'But his reflection is dangerous. Is yours?'

'Och no. My fantasies are well within the norm. Unlike yours.'

'Mine were overmagnified.'

She smiled to herself and ran her fingers though her thick mousy hair, smug in the knowledge that she knew better. The vulnerability that I had seen in her before was nowhere to be seen now. It had served its purpose. Instead, there was a tough creature with bright, calculating eyes, softly rolling her hard Rs, reeling me in.

'The disks were to frighten me.'

'Of course.'

'I have a third.'

'Oh?'

'One from Pornoland.'

The confidence in her eyes faltered for a moment as if she was working something out. 'You played?' she said.

'Yes.'

'Up to what level?'

'Enough to win me. I didn't see you eating the banana.'

'Don't be stupid, I was never there.'

'So why was David?'

'We were working something out. You're Cabbie, then?'

'Yes,' I lied, and I had a feeling that she was too, about David.

She smiled, to herself again. 'You do surprise me. You do indeed. Well, in that case, you owe the game's banker some money.'

'£250,000?'

'That's right.'

'You are joking now.'

'No.'

'Well, you've got my card number.'

'Not any more.'

It was my turn to falter. Warren must have wiped it when he poked around the system. Typical.

She leaned over the table and inspected her smooth, long, unvarnished nails with their white crescent moons. 'What did you think of the sequence? Had to use a different body, of course. Yours is, well . . .' she said.

'Some people like it.'

She didn't like that, and made no further comment. I waited, wondering whether or not it was a reasonable question to ask, and then said: 'How come I lost?'

'Played out of character. Always fatal, that. You knew David well enough. But I suppose you couldn't face killing yourself. Understandable, but awful silly. It is only a game, after all.'

'I thought there might be another option.'

'For him? Och no. Cabbie has to kill, in the end.'

'It was the chopping that threw me. My experience is that he likes to choke.'

She stared at me with undisguised hostility and I felt a strange thrill. Warren had gone down the tube for £250,000 because he couldn't face killing me. Not even in fun. David could, but not Warren, not Cabbie. What a sweetie. He didn't intend to pay, of course, but it was the principle of the thing.

'You videoed me at IPEX, didn't you?' I said.

'Yes.'

'Did you follow us?'

'To where? The cloakroom? Or the hotel?'

'Did you?'

'No. Why should I?'

I wanted to say that maybe he'd told her to, like she said he'd told her to deliver the disks, but I felt pity for her and guilt was still revolving inside me. I couldn't get away from it. I'd messed around with her husband, and had paid.

'I didn't know he was married,' I said.

'But when you did, you didn't stop, did you?' she replied.

'No. But I have tried.'

'You should never have started, not with my David.'

'I thought it was a game, between the two of us. People play games, for fun, a thrill, you know . . .'

'Game well and truly on.'

'I believe it. So, who's winning?'

She clenched her teeth to stop herself telling me too much, her strong jaw setting a smooth, hard line round her face. It was for her to know and me to find out. I searched in my bag for a fresh pack of twenty. There wasn't an ashtray on the bright, nut-brown table but I lit up all the same. The smoke drifted over her head as I spoke. Time to teach her some manners.

'Well, Julie, how about this? I've got proof that

Pornoland exists. I've got the nasty little animation of me, and I played the game this morning long enough to get printouts that would give . . . a flavour of what goes down between your punters. One, the number can be traced to here. Two, David, your husband's onscreen. Three, JJ 1000 is obviously yours, a test site for Babylon. Four, you get the number for Pornoland from there. Five, I've walked round your system and read your mail. I've got enough to prove you're the Sysop and to bury you.'

In computing terms, the Sysop is the systems operator, God – not a TLA, the real thing – and if he (and experience shows that, like God, it usually is he) didn't exactly create the system, he certainly runs it from above. Everything that appears on the board appears with his say-so, and you can't hide from the Sysop because he is a super-user, which means he can poke his nose in anywhere he likes and wipe you out – if he's got the time, and the inclination.

She shrugged her narrow shoulders and pushed her chair back. Her hands felt under the table and pulled out a drawer. She put her hands inside and drew out a clean crystal ashtray which she slid towards me along the table top.

'Big deal. Say I am. My bulletin board is packed with stuff and there's nothing to stop someone else running a section with a game on it. Someone plays a game, gives you a number to call. That's nothing to do with me. I just manage the show. I can't be expected to monitor every little bit. How do I know what people are doing in scrambled parts of my system? Some files are divided up, with itty bitty names, so they'd make no sense even if I did peek in.'

She was right. It was possible to be a closed conference user on someone else's bulletin board. It was possible that the game from which Warren had earned the Pornoland number had been set up by someone else. It was possible that Pornoland was run by someone else on her machine. That's what bulletin boards were for, for people to stick in their stuff and share it. In this instance, it just wasn't probable.

'It's the only show on your system. And it is your system,' I said.

'JJ 1000 is my system.'

'Your personal files are on another machine. The same machine that runs Pornoland.'

'Are they?'

'Yes.'

'My personal files are all I work with. I have a small bulletin board on it through a link to the university. The game you describe could be an invisible option. I could only access it if I knew it was there. And I don't.'

'How do you intend to explain your phone line being tied up all hours of the day?'

'My university link. Next?'

It was tough going and she knew it. It was going to be hard to prove that she had set the whole thing up and not some fly-by-night gamester using her system. I had a story, but I didn't have her, and that's what I really wanted. I took my time over the cigarette. She waited patiently until I had crushed the stub into the glass before pushing back her chair and standing. I watched her smoothing down her white T-shirt over a white denim skirt. She wasn't tall, and she had heavier breasts and wider, rounder hips than I. She also had a suntan, which looked fake. It struck me as funny. Maybe she'd tried to protect herself in the same, simple way that I had. I tried to remember how she'd looked before, when she came crying to me about her phoney disks. I wanted to know what I'd missed. The fact was, I hadn't liked her then, but guilt had got in the way of good judgement. That was my speciality, a good shot to the foot. I got up as she opened the door. I pictured David by her side. How had she survived?

'Why do it, Julie?' I said.

She walked over and pressed her hands down and around my dress. When she was satisfied that I wasn't wired up, she said: 'Why set you up?'

'I know why you did that. Why . . .'

'. . . would someone like me run a game like that?'

'Yes.'

'For the money, why else?'

I followed her down the grey-carpeted corridor and opened a wood-veneered door into a large room with a chequerboard floor and a couple of high quality computer workstations. On a shelf, by one wall, was a row of what seemed to be flying helmets with built-in visors and several pairs of cabled motorcyclists's gloves. At the end of the shelf were clothes hangers with two black suits hanging from them.

'D'ye want to jack in? I'll take the smaller suit,' she said, lifting up her T-shirt and hanging it on a hook. She unzipped her skirt, let it fall, and lifted one bulky black sheath from its hanger. She put it on like a wet suit, stepping into the flexible leggings and pushing her arms into the sleeves. With one tug, she pulled on a strap that zipped the suit up at the back.

'Jack into what?' I said.

'David's virtual reality machine. Graphics like you've never seen. Best money can buy. Put on the suit and stay in the squared-off area. It's a treat I saved for the end.'

I tugged my denim shirt over my head. In for a penny, I thought . . .

'The scarf. Better take it off,' she said, pointing.

I fingered the scarf and untied it, reluctantly. Though the bruises were not so livid, I still felt self-conscious of them, as if they were glow-in-the-dark markers of what I'd let him do. She didn't help by staring first at my neck and then at my small naked breasts. I stared back defiantly until she turned away to rummage on the shelf for something. It was a jar of Vaseline.

'The suit might rub your nipples. Put this on. The guys use it,' she said.

'Pass,' I said, handing the jar back and nodding at the suit. It was a little large for me but comfortable all the same, a soft, warm exoskeleton of Lycra and wire. Julie took the cable tail that ran down my spine and connected it to a box by one computer screen. I felt a moment of tension as she did this, as if 10,000 volts might surge down the line and seize up my vitals. Nothing happened. She plugged herself into a second socket and handed me a helmet.

As soon as I placed it on my head and pulled the wraparound visor over my eyes, she disappeared, and a distant, shadowy figure took her place. The room we stood in was transformed into a bare landscape of marble and stone. A row of marble arches, as finely drawn as an architect's exercise in perspective, stood against a cobalt blue sky, too perfect for clouds. As I turned my heavy head towards the dark body which danced in and out of the columns, the image rotated to my point of view. I had no idea what to do.

'Move your legs,' said a voice. It was Julie's. 'Catch me,' she said.

I stepped forward very slowly, lumbering like a blindfolded player in a game of buff. At one point, I must have walked to the edge of the square because a chasm two miles deep opened up at my feet and I started backwards from the edge of the sheer cliff, my heart pounding hard and fast.

'Turn around. You can do better than that.'

I turned my head to face the sound of her voice and the figure I had tried to follow stood before me. I reached out and, though a hand touched her shoulder, I felt nothing.

My virtual hand had touched the slim naked form of a tall woman but couldn't feel her pale skin, the shape of her bones, the tone of her muscles or the heat of her body. She had long, dark hair in unkempt switches over her angular shoulders. Her breasts were small and her hips boyishly narrow. Her greyish mouth was generous and her nose slightly hooked, her eyes blue under dark brows. She was smiling at me. I was not smiling at me. It was me.

'Surprised?' said the voice and the mouth of my image moved.

'What's going on?' I said.

'I'm lifting my hand,' she said. The image of me waved. 'Look, I can even scratch my fanny,' she said and the shameless image of me did the same. 'I can do lots of things.'

'I bet,' I said.

'Want me to bend over?'

'No, thanks.'

She did anyway. The anatomical detail was cruel. I heard a clicking sound and the view grew in magnification.

'OK, you be you. Do you want force-feedback?'

'What's that?'

'It allows you to feel the images that you touch or that touch you. I'm switching the cables.'

The screen wrapped around my eyes went blank and then jumped up again into the three-dimensional stereoscopic vision I had seen before. This time there was no image of me standing under the timeless arches, but one of David.

'Look down,' she said.

I did, and there on the floor was a gun. There was a rope and knife too. They seemed as accessible as pennies in a pool.

Julie grew impatient. 'Pick one up, then.'

I stepped forward, feeling the hard tile of the floor beneath, and picked up the gun. It was heavy.

'Och, you're no fun. Pick up the rope.'

I dropped the gun, fumbling as I stooped, my real hand grasping at nothing, my virtual hand pale as a grey glove in moonlight, ghosted away from me in space. I touched the rope and clenched my fist around it, feeling the sinewy weight twist heavily in my hand, ungovernable as a live snake.

'Throw the rope to me.'

I threw the rope, which rotated high up between the arches before settling at her – his feet. He stooped to pick it up and walked slowly towards me, pulling the rope tight between the fists of his hands. I stood motionless as David came closer, wan and smooth-skinned, waxing to the edges of the visor so that I could see deep into the empty, dark space of his eyes. Quadrophonic breathing, rough as a saw, echoed in my ears and something began to tighten around my throat, which tensed against the suit's multitudinous air pockets inflating like balloons and stiffening with pressure and force. The crotch of my suit began to warm and vibrate until I felt pleasure at my own strangulation. As I choked for air, I could hear her, cursing and cursing me to hell and flames.

Somehow I concentrated my true senses enough to rip off my helmet and emerged gasping like a beached fish. She was laughing now, hands on her hips, and the pressure had gone from my neck. I stared around frantically for the rope but there wasn't anything there, just the computers displaying a man and a woman, standing together in an arched courtyard. Julie was standing fully rigged out in her data suit, the rows of dead helmets behind her.

'You've just lost your head,' she said, looking to the side with the air of a foraging beetle, seeing only what her visor showed her. She lifted her hands to her head and eased off her helmet.

'Any good? No? Well, it's not quite accurate. He had to texture-map images of you on to polygons, which is not as satisfactory as a three-dimensional scan, but you were hardly going to sit still for that, were you? No matter, the machine's powerful enough to make it very realistic, don't you think?'

'Why me?' I said.

'Come on, grow up, why don't you? It's custom-built. It's the inflatable doll of the future. Barbie and Ken for grown-ups. All this . . .' she said, waving her hand around the room, '. . . is the prototype for a virtual sex machine. A testing ground for teledildonics and custom-made fantasies. Look at the suits, the pressure pads. Not quite as satisfying as the real thing, I'll wager, but at least a dream can never be spoiled by a crappy suntan and a cheap haircut.'

I wondered how she could be so cool about the whole thing, and how it was that I could have been taken in by her initial act. I couldn't be so wrong about everything. I wasn't. I knew David, and he was twisted but never false. He was true. He couldn't say it, but I knew he was jealous and possessive. He didn't want me for display, but for himself. He'd made everything that I'd just experienced. I believed that, but I couldn't believe her blithe acceptance of it. The digitized video of me in Pornoland couldn't have been his idea. It had to be hers. She'd done it for spite. She was jealous too. I bet she put him in Pornoland too, for spite, which meant maybe he didn't know about it.

'Do you play the part of me? You know, when you two come in here?' I said.

She turned away and clattered her helmet on the shelf. Her answer said neither yes nor no. 'Anyone can play any part. You can even play on your own, with the computer taking over the other party though that makes it a bit predictable. Computers aren't like people,' she said, keeping her back to me.

'I want it wiped.'

'You can set the force-feedback to whatever parameters you require, or switch it off. You might like it better that way since there is no pain. There'd be no nasty little welts or bruises, either.'

'I want it wiped.'

'Sorry.'

'I'll call the police.'

'Call them. It'll do no good. This is part of a bona fide pyscho-sexual project. All above board, medical stuff, research funding and all that. This is just a piece of it, there are many scenarios to choose from. You're spoilt for choice here. It's a veritable sexual Woolworths – no, considering the cost, it has to be Harrods.'

I'm not a violent person but I badly wanted to hit her. I wanted to slap her about and throw her to the floor, I wanted to kick her and kick her and stamp on her head. As she tugged the strap down her back and shook her arms out of the stiff sleeves, I knew that I would have done better kicking myself.

'What if I told him about Pornoland?' I said.

She bit her lip as she sized me up. 'He knows about it. We're a team. I handle games, he handles fantasy,' she said. She kept on talking while she put her clothes on, her back to me. 'Aren't you impressed by his work here? It links a lot of technologies. Interactive video, neuro-programming, parallel processing and virtual reality.'

'To what end?'

'Surrogate sexual experience. David got a lot of sponsorship for it. You know, the electronic rhino horn, programming sexual potency. If you haven't got it, he can replicate it. You don't have to be old or disabled any more. If you can't walk, run or feel, if you can't get it up, come to him and he'll put you inside a machine where you can do it all. David's working on feedback from the machine, stimulation of the whole body, all those erogenous zones, including, of course, the brain. It's an advance in medical science.'

'I can see that. But what's your interest? Its potential in the marital aid industry?' I raised my fingers in the air to describe quotation marks.

'Of course.'

'It's hardly ethical.'

'I think we're beyond worrying about computers and ethics, aren't we?' she said.

'So where does the pyschobabble come in?'

'Fantasies. He's working with sexual behavioural therapists, offering a black box that does the business. Eroticism is a mental, not a physical thing, an intensely personal interpretation of action. David's working on software that will enable users to build and explore their fantasies so they don't have to just work at them inside their heads with the help of dirty books and tapes. They experience them, outside their own minds – in virtual reality. He's awful clever.'

'So who're your main customers, apart from the poor sods who can't get it up any more?'

'The ones who can. And how. Rapists, child molesters, sadists . . . deviants, you know. The core of the project is treatment, by sexually conditioning the user to control his own behaviour. That's what David got the money for.'

'How does it work?'

'A user can be conditioned to react to fantasies he or she creates within the computer. Alternatively, the user can be forced not to react.'

'How?'

'Satiation. Too much of the desired object. It's taken

over from aversion therapy in the treatment of sex offenders.'

'It doesn't work with cigarettes,' I said, but she ignored me.

'Virtech is creating effective desensitizing sexual scenarios through virtual reality . . .'

I didn't like the word desensitize. It was OK when you were talking about hay fever, but when you were talking about sex it reminded me of clitoridectomies, archiodectomies, lobotomies – cuts, cuts, cuts.

'. . . A male paedophile probably never had a positive response from a woman. He can get one with this machine. He can always get one with this machine, in a structured, realistic, normal fantasy, that is, within the bounds of what society deems is normal.'

'How does he come if he likes kids and not women?'

'They make him. C'mon, I don't have to draw you a picture, do I? He has to peak during a normal fantasy, then he is rewarded with a fantasy about kids, over and over again. Outcome. He doesn't come for what he likes best. Frankly . . .'

'It bores him rigid.'

'Senseless. They destroy the part of the deviant fantasy that really turns him on. Or they let him experience the deviant fantasy and focus on the part that really arouses him, offering it to him, post-orgasm . . .'

'Spoil that for him, too. Very good. How do they find out what really turns someone on?'

'Sensors measure the arousal through pupil dilation, fluctuations in temperature, heart rate and organ volume change. He has to go over and over it. That's sensors with an s, by the way,' she said, and laughed.

'What about women?'

'There aren't as many deviant women, frankly. It should work for them too. No reason why not. There could be a spin-off in erotic fantasies for frigid women,

135

but as far as treatment is concerned, the main thrust is in treating men, impotent men, disabled men, deviant men.'

'How much to kill it? The one of me. How much?'

'Och, he'd never do that. It's worth a lot to Virtech. It's worth a lot to him.'

'What about you? How much is it worth to you?'

'Let's see. How about £250,000? That should cover it, if you don't mind the risk.'

'What risk?'

'That David would be very upset.'

'Let him be upset.'

'Smash it to pieces if you want, then,' she said. 'Go on. But remember one thing, if he doesn't have this, he'll have to have you. Won't he?'

She pulled sharply at the cables and I stood there like the ghost of a stormtrooper, a helmeted head, which seemed more real than my own, under my arm. My brain might as well have been. What could I do? I had quite a bit in the bank but not that much. She wanted payment in full and there was only one place to go for that, to the person who owed her.

She leaned over the keyboard. The screen showed the scene I had viewed through the visor. The arched courtyard was empty, the sky blue and cloudless. She tapped in an instruction and another image of my naked body revolved in the inner space of the computer. She pressed another button and David's body whirled around. The proportions were so accurate that it almost hurt to look at the palms of his hands, the soles of his feet, the swirls of his fair hair, and the heavy-headed loll of his penis. She picked up a heavy black cabled glove and slipped her soft hand into it. The hand that appeared on the screen was as real as her own. The only thing that betrayed the falsehood was its own perfection. As she flexed the glove, the scenery on screen began to move until there, by a surrealistic window, stood the image of me, the disembodied hand flying towards it, resting on my shoulder like a flesh-coloured bird. Julie caressed the real air and jerked her hand forward. With the same sharp movement, the woman that I was fell forward and out of the window.

'He plays with this thing for hours,' she said, and the screen went blank with one sharp tap of her finger. 'I'll see you outside.'

I placed the helmet gently on its shelf and tugged at the strap on my back. He'd told me all about it. I was nothing till he made me. He could call me up and chase me through fake chasms that he had created, hunt me like a deer through a bright-lined forest. He could place his virtual hands around my skinny virtual neck and squeeze. He could stab me with a virtual knife, shoot me with a virtual gun, put himself inside the virtual dead, see and feel it, just the way he'd always wanted to. I could die a hundred times and more for him and she wanted £250,000 to make him stop. But what if he did stop, what then? He'd come for me. She had said he would and I was sure of that. The maniac would come for me. This way he had me for ever. I tied the scarf around my neck and picked up my dress.

'Keep it. I don't care what he does in software so long as he stays away from me,' I said, pushing against the glass door to the outside.

'You still owe £250,000,' she said.

'Whistle for it. I told you. Think of it as my fee for keeping your husband happy.'

The door swung to in my face and I saw her press buttons in a wall to lock it tight. She had a big smile on her face.

CHAPTER TWELVE

I parked the car and hurried up the steps of the dark house to open the front door. There was no light in the lounge or from Richard's bedroom. He'd still be in the pub, red-nosed and red-eyed over one pint too many, crying into his beer over Diane Shine, his fantasy woman, sleek and black and cheeky, jumping from bed to bed depending on who she thought could lift her up the slippery ladder to success.

I'd had a lot of time to think, driving hard down the motorway. I had a story now all right, but did I want to write it? Did I want to write about the virtual sex machine at Virtech? Did I ever. I could, and I didn't even have to mention the bit about David using the system for himself, not as healer attempting to heal himself. He'd had himself well and truly analysed, I'll bet, just to make sure it was really good. The place was probably crawling with psychiatrists on a good day.

Pornoland was a bonus. That was a fine scandal. Top gamester prostituting her talents and faking sex scenes involving innocent bystanders, i.e. me. Run the story with her denials. Peddling porn. It was certainly less honourable than pyscho-sexual therapy for sex offenders. I had my money on her. She was on to something big. The game had gone down this morning, but it had to come up again: there was money being made on this, big-time gambling money. If Warren owed £250,000, the stakes were high. There was one thing that kept me from calling my news desk right away. Right now I was a toy in her husband's sex machine. She could embarrass me with the truth about why I was there, and she could scare me with the thought that with a press of a button I need not be.

I wished Richard had been home. I didn't like standing on the wrong side of the front door, rattling my keys in the locks. I needed a drink, badly. I could feel my lips puckering at the thought of a shot that would burn down my throat and sting my stomach. I wanted a rush of well-being through my veins instead of a goosestepping march of fear up my spine. David had made me afraid of the dark, of things in my mind.

As the last key turned in the last lock, the telephone began to ring. I held the edge of the door, waiting and watching the telephone in the gloomy hallway. Say it was him, calling me, checking that I was at home? Maybe she'd told him I'd been. She could stir him up and make him come to me. I switched on the light, waited for four rings and heard Richard's recorded message click into action. Diane Shine's breathless voice all but elbowed its way past the tone.

'Georgina, Diane. It's 10.30. p.m. I went up to Virtech with Warren to see Julie Jones. We saw David Jones too. They had a fight. He's coming for you. Wait there and I'll be over with Richard. Wait there.'

Panic tingled like static over my body. Who'd had a fight? Who was coming for me? Wait here? No fear.

I ran to pick up the phone but she'd gone. How could I wait? If I waited, he'd get me. If I didn't and left, they'd think he had. What the hell was I supposed to do now? I'd switched on the light because I'd been afraid of the dark. Now, I was alone in a bright hallway like a joker in the limelight. I had to switch off that light again and hide in the shadows so I'd be safe in the dark that I was afraid of. I prayed that Wonderwoman, in the shape of dippy Diane, would possibly realize that I was hiding, and whoever was coming to get me would think I hadn't arrived yet.

A car drove up fast and stopped with a judder of metal and rubber. A door opened and slammed. I didn't hear footsteps but I could see the front door. I hadn't shut it. I started like a skater across the polished wooden floor, slithering to push the door shut and lock out the looming terror. I moved my whole bodyweight forward on the inside, and felt the door resist. His hands were on it already, pushing against it. I should have screamed but I was working too hard with what muscle I had to shut that door. My feet began to slide away from me, lengthening, stretching, slipping along the parquet. With my eyes squeezed shut and my teeth gritted, I couldn't think of anyone worth calling for, except God and Mummy, Mummy, Mummy. I should have known better. The door swung wide open and I was thrown back against the wall with some force.

'Get in the fucking car,' he said, leaning forward and grabbing hold of my arm. His brown fingers squeezed the muscle down to the bone and his crazy eyes were open wide, the whites showing like curved teeth around steel holes.

'Warren . . .'

The rest of what I had to say I swallowed as he jerked me forward, hauled and hustled me down the steps to his car, a red, soap-shaped, big-litre Sierra. He ducked me down into the front seat with a hard hand to the back of my head and stumbled over the bonnet in an effort to get over to the driver's door. I was trying to strap myself in when the car took off, burning rubber like a dragster, and he swung a left at the roundabout, two hundred yards down the road.

'Take it easy, for Chrissakes,' I said, my voice breaking

as my hands slammed on to the dashboard and my shoulder against the side door as I strove to stay in my seat. The Sierra was accelerating down a narrow road so that cars and yellow skips flew past like planets and stars in a space odyssey. It lurched to the left and to the right as Warren took short cuts and double backs towards the Bow flyover, from which I thought we would take off and spin to oblivion like Campbell's Bluebird. He drove like a joyrider, weaving from lane to lane and hurtling across lights. I waited in vain for the sound of sirens in pursuit of the speeding car, which had broken every limit through five miles of late-night traffic.

When we hit what appeared to be open road between two huge tracts of common land, he went faster. My fingers gripped the soft, velvety upholstery of the seat as Warren rammed his foot down to the floor. As we approached a pair of mini roundabouts, I discovered I hadn't breathed out for a while. Warren pulled hard right on the wheel, cutting fast across a line of oncoming traffic. There was the sound of angry horns and then silence along a fresh stretch of road that separated a collection of low-rise blocks and an estate of handsome Victorian houses from a wide stretch of parkland. Warren glanced in the mirror and wrenched the car to the right again, pulling up the hand-brake fast so that the Sierra swivelled to a skid-pan halt on the bone-shaking gravel of rough ground by a lake.

He killed the lights and I stared out at a pair of swans, white in the moonless night, gliding quickly away to the safety of a shadowy island. I could hear my rapid breathing and Warren's. His hands gripped the wheel and then jerked open the door. I waited a moment before gently pulling back the handle on my side. All I did was touch his shoulder and say, 'Mr Graham, we won't bother with the Highway Code, I'm afraid you have failed . . .'

He swung round and clipped me twice around the head. 'You bleedin' idiot,' he said, swinging his hands at me again.

I took two more blows and went for him. I hit him as hard and as often as I could until I realized he had stopped hitting me a while back and was simply fending off my hysterical attack. I dropped my hands and he walked away to hammer his fists on the Sierra's glinting roof.

'You stupid, stupid bitch.'

'What? What? What? Tell me what?' I yelled.

'Why him, eh? Why d'ya let him? Fucking nut-nut.'

I didn't reply because he wasn't about to listen. Warren had things to say. He swore and blathered while I leaned patiently against the car bonnet, arms folded, my eyes rolling heavenwards with every fresh accusation.

'What do you know?' I said, when he stopped to take a breather.

He held his long-fingered hands wide apart and chopped them downwards as if to steady himself and his thoughts. 'OK, OK,' he said, breathing deeply. 'Diane asked me to go with her. I said OK. I wanted to nose around anyway. We see this Julie bird. Diane tries the game story on her. No way. Tough as boot leather. We see her old man. He knew me. He knew. Want to try something you never had, he said? I said yeah, why not? I gets rigged out in a data suit and we jack in.'

'To what?'

'Some interactive porn shit with you as the fucking star. Why'd you do it? Let them do it? It's happening all over again, all over again. You're up to your neck in something you know fuck all about.'

'And you do, do you?'

'Don't you care?'

I turned away to look at the swans but they'd disappeared, leaving slow ripples on the brown water that spread out to a thin rim of sandy shingle and a grass-tufted edge. A plastic bag rested, half submerged, a bloated corner sticking up like the fin of a small white shark.

'It wasn't real,' I said.

'You don't get it, do you?'

'I do get it.'

'You fucking like that stuff?'

'No.'

'So why?'

'He made it up. He made it all up. It's me, yes, but it's in his brain. I had nothing to do with that.'

'I don't believe you.'

'Why do I have to explain to you? You turn up after all these years like some forgotten Smartie, sticking yourself into things that are just not your business. What's it to you? I know you tricked me with all that buddy-buddy stuff this weekend, so that Diane could get ahead of me.'

'You don't half talk some shit. I flew half way across the world because I thought you were in trouble.'

'Well, I am now. Why'd you leave with her? Why'd you leave the hotel?'

'I turned up at her place after I had a visit from your friendly copper.'

'Falk?'

'Yeah. Popped in for a chat. Told me to piss off, basically.'

He stopped speaking but he didn't stop moving. He kept nodding, his hands slapping the top of the car. Then he wiped his hand over his face and held it over his mouth. 'I could have done what I wanted. Do you know what he can do with that machine?'

'It isn't me. For Chrissakes, Warren. He's painted a picture of a fantasy and made it happen outside his head. But it isn't real. It's a fake. It's his way of keeping in control. I tried to explain to you yesterday, how it all happened.'

'I could touch you and feel you. Understand? I could touch you. When you touched me I could feel it. Inside.'

'I get the picture, don't go on.'

'You don't understand, George. I wanted to. I wanted to so bad.'

'So why didn't you? Jack in and jerk off.'

That deserved a slap but Warren stood silently with his head down, leaning into the car, one leg bent, arms above the passenger door. I could hear intermittent traffic behind me, and something sliding into the water, breaking the surface tension with a cold slippery splash. Warren's silence damned him.

'Well, bully for you, you little shit,' I said, pushing myself away from the car.

I walked down to the lake. That's all I needed, a man with a dicky conscience coming at me like a lunatic with smoking matches under his toes. David had put him on fast spin and hung him out to dry. No wonder Diane was half hysterical on the phone. What a good story she had, my story, if she could get her head round it.

Warren came and stood beside me. 'It's a weird experience, George.'

'Making love to me, or wanking in a suit?'

'Come on. I didn't.'

'Oh, really? What stopped you? Needed customizing, did it?'

'The body bag is about as subtle as a Russian condom, and the graphics, well, they're good but not that good.'

'So write it up for *Computer Shopper*. Parallel processing isn't all it's cracked up to be. Buyer beware.'

'I'm talking about the effing principle of something here.'

He stamped off across the gravel to the car, stopped

dead and stamped all the way back. He half crouched, swinging his arms outwards in frustration.

'Ain't you never loved no one?'

I placed my fingers to my mouth and tried to think. I'd loved my husband Eddie and a fat lot of good that had been. In a weak moment, a long time ago, I'd thought that I loved Warren. He'd almost got me again this time. They had both double-crossed me in the end, but that was another story. The truth was that seeing Warren again had been one of the better things that had happened to me this summer and I would have preferred that Diane had stuck to her first choice, Richard, and left Warren to me. We had some making up to do, he was looking so good, and he did get so worked up about me. But it was too late now, I saw no point in confessions.

'It's been so long, I can't quite remember,' I said.

'All I ever wanted was you.'

'And the money.'

'And the money.'

'So you got the money. Half a loaf and all that. I've lived a life since you skipped with the swagbag,' I said, kicking a stone into the water and walking away from him round the stony edge.

He shouted after me – 'A rotten fucking life' – and then started after me. He came up quickly, swung me around, grabbed my chin and pushed me backwards.

'You like this, huh?' he said. He pulled my face forward and pushed it back roughly, squeezing my chin tightly. 'You like it, huh? You want it rough, huh?'

I gripped his hand. 'Don't.'

'Don't? Come on. You should've said, babe. I could have been rough with you. Real rough.'

'Warren, you couldn't rough up a sandpit if it wore a skirt. Behave.'

Warren said, 'Shit,' and looked away. He stuck his hands into his jeans pockets so his shoulders were all hunched up and stiff. We stood looking over the dark water that glimmered with the orange glow of the street lamps. The summer breeze from the dark scrubland around was warm and humid, holding moisture like a foetid sponge. There was nothing fresh about the stifling air, nothing crisp, clean or sharp. It was suffocating.

'Someone'd paid me a visit. Been in my room, through my things,' he said.

'Anything missing?'

'I had a weapon.'

'A weapon? A gun. And it's gone?'

'Yeah.'

'When?'

'When I was with you.'

'Who? You know who?'

The way his shoulders stayed hunched up, I knew he wasn't going to tell me no matter how badly I wanted – needed – to know. I changed the subject.

'Well, I've had some fun too. While you were feeling the virtual earth move, I took a trip to Pornoland.'

'Yeah?'

'You didn't win. You lost.'

'Yeah.'

'Why'd you choose him?'

'The black guys had regular profiles. Big dicks. Street-wise. Pimp material. He looked like a winner.'

'Liar. You'd never have gone for him. You'd seen him before, hadn't you?'

'I read about him. Yeah.'

'My piece?'

'Yeah.'

'You look out for my stuff?' I was touched.

'I subscribe.'

'Oh, that it? So why couldn't you do what he wanted? It was only a game.'

'Yeah. But it ain't no game now.'

I looked up at him. There wasn't a mark on him, that I could see. No swelling about the face, no bruises on the arms. He had dark marks on his T-shirt.

'So what did you do? Kill him?'

'I gave him a slap, that's all.'

'Lucky you didn't have a – weapon.'

'Lucky for him.'

I turned and walked across the gravel and dirt to the car. As I opened the door, I yelled over to him. 'By the way, what do you think?'

'What?'

I pointed at my head.

'You do it for a bet, or what?' he said.

Bastard, and I thought blondes had more fun.

'What now?' I said, hungry for a cigarette as he slid into the driver's seat. My handbag was in the hall back home.

'What time you got?'

'Late.'

'I'll take you home. Tomorrow, we go to Virtech. No way he's keeping that shit on his machine.'

'I'd rather it stayed where it was.'

'No way.'

'Look, if it keeps him away from me, let him have it.'

'No way.'

'Warren, give it a rest. This isn't the movies. I'm not your girl. You don't have to save me.'

'Oh, but I do, babe. This time, you're going to make the right choice.'

I sat with my legs crossed and my arms folded tightly across my chest as Warren turned the key in the ignition. He seemed to be thinking. After about a minute, he leaned over and put his hand behind my neck. I tensed, but didn't pull away. I stayed just as I was, tight and wrapped up, looking into those greenish, dark-lashed eyes until he closed them and bent his head over my face.

I kept my eyes wide open while my lips received his kiss, a fifteen-second miracle of sensuality and restraint. If I'd closed my eyes I'd have been in danger of tuning into what was running through Warren's mind. I decided not to go along for the ride, this time.

His lips disengaged with a moist pop and he sighed, like a man weary of chocolates that never yielded quite the taste he desired. Without a word, he put the car slowly into gear and it crept with a gentle crunch back on to the road. He chose a different route back to my place, driving more sanely this time. We were stopped once and Warren had to show his hire car papers, his driving licence and his passport to a humourless cop who kept asking if I was all right. It was plain that the make and engine capacity of the car were out of keeping for a man like Warren. The policeman would have felt happier if it had been a five-year-old Datsun Cherry, but he did let us go when he was satisfied with the papers. He even called Warren 'sir'.

Half way home we came to some lights on amber, and Warren pulled into the yellow-lined box and indicated right. Straight ahead was a large white Peugeot which had stopped on red. There were two white men in their mid-twenties in the front and two in the back. They all had razor-sharp haircuts, gelled into monk-like fringes. The driver tapped his gold-ringed hand to music that the rest were pushing their heads back and forward to. I looked straight at them and they stared right back. They didn't smile. They chewed imaginary gum and pumped their jaws to the beat.

'What's up with them?' I said, as Warren turned the car.

'White girl, black guy, big motor. Not on, my son. Should've sat in the back, babe, then I'd have looked like your driver.'

I didn't answer. I looked across at Warren to say

something nice and saw the white car pull quickly alongside. Warren kept his eyes on the road.

'Warren . . .' I said.

'I clocked 'em,' he replied and we accelerated away. The Peugeot dropped behind as Warren kept his toe down. When he reached a higgledy-piggledy high street of small shops and a couple of late-night snack bars, he braked, swung left and then straightened up fast.

'Shit. No through,' he said, manoeuvring the gears into reverse as the Peugeot forced the car into the kerb against a huddle of black plastic rubbish bags and cardboard boxes. Warren tried to drive the car forward, round the Peugeot and into the road, but it was too late, there was nowhere to go except right there.

He swore and leaned over me to click down the lock on my door. His was already being wrenched open. The two guys that had been in the front were so quick that he didn't have a chance to turn and face them before they'd caught his legs. As they dragged him out on to the road, his chin caught the steering wheel with a bone-jarring thud. I tried to scramble over to the driver's seat to grab him back but he was already out and gripping the door. As the two men twisted his body, and he struggled to push the door back shut, a beefy ginger-haired yob in a black polyester tracksuit that billowed like a parachute got hold of Warren's head. A gold-ringed fist smashed into Warren's mouth and blood oozed through his white teeth. The car shook, someone rattled the door on my side and I began to scream.

Somehow, as Warren was dragged away behind the car, he freed a leg and kicked the driver's door shut. I could hear him shouting to me to lock it, lock it, lock it.

I panicked. If I locked it, he wouldn't be able to get back in, if I didn't, they'd get me. I looked one way and another, through the windscreen, through the windows, until I couldn't see him any more. Mumbling to myself like some lunatic, I stretched up to look behind and I could see the upper bodies of three of them. They were twisting their hips, arms out like footballers, kicking hard at something on the ground. One spare man walked quickly past the windows towards the driver's door. I couldn't see his face, just the violet wrinkles of his two-tone fashion jacket. I leaned over fast and pushed down the lock, knocking the car-phone from its cradle in the process. His pale, greasy face pressed against the glass as I dialled and the car yawed like a boat in a storm. I couldn't hear clearly, but I knew well enough what his metal-filled mouth was saying. Nigger lover. Nigger lover. Nigger lover. It was far too late to explain that Warren and I were just good friends. I didn't want to answer back. I just wished that I was a big, hairy gorilla of a man – with a weapon.

Long before the sirens sounded, they'd gone. Some short, stocky, Turkish-looking men in polyester polo shirts and slightly flared slacks had come out from the snack bar to stand over me, and watch the blood bubble from Warren's mouth over the dusty, pitted tarmac. Seems like they'd called the police, too, but I couldn't understand what they were saying to each other. I was on my knees, talking like a monkey through chattering teeth, talking to Warren, who couldn't answer me. Under the pulse of blue lights, I followed the stretcher and his bloodied, bobbing head, his eyes swollen shut, his face split like a ripe watermelon on a white plate. Someone put a long comfortable arm around my shoulder and I cried and cried into the cold, silver buttons of a blue-uniformed chest.

CHAPTER THIRTEEN

I didn't get home until just before dawn and then I couldn't sleep. I'd left Warren in a mess of tubes and bandages, and the police with the number of the Peugeot and a statement. They said they'd contact the hire company.

I was in the kitchen drinking coffee when Diane passed by the door on the way to the bathroom. She stopped.

'Is that you, Georgina?'

I didn't reply.

'Are you all right?'

'Not really.'

'He went crazy. I tried to warn you. Did you get the message?'

'Yeah, thanks. Coffee?' I said.

She looked down the hall towards Richard's bedroom and said: 'Please.'

I poured what remained in the cafetière into a mug and stuck it in the microwave.

'OK, what do we know?' I said, sitting back down. The microwave pinged and she took out her coffee, holding Richard's shiny, red, quilted dressing gown tight against her nakedness.

'Well, Julie Jones was a waste of time.'

'Well, if you hadn't been in such a hurry to beat me to this story, you might have got a bit more,' I said.

'I didn't think you were about to share.'

'No, you're right. But I might have been if you hadn't been so . . . Oh, I'm sorry, go on.'

'I think we should call the police.'

'And tell them what?' I said.

'Warren said David Jones threatened you. Tell the police. Tell them he frightens you.'

'Big deal. He shouldn't have told you anything.'

'Tell them this man's assaulted you.'

'Did he?'

'OK. Tell them about the porn game.'

'What game? Soon as you told her, she pulled the plug.'

Diane sat opposite me, her coffee mug in her two hands, her long, brown, creamy-nailed fingers crossed in front. She put the mug down carefully and took a deep breath. 'That story's still alive, George.'

'I know that. I can run it on what I've got. I played the game before it went down. I've got proof it existed at least. Tell me about MT Industries.'

'OK. We in this together?'

'Together.'

She told me that she had found something in the piece that I had written about Virtech after I had first met David. The company was banking on two big orders when I wrote about it. When Diane had made her connections via the IPEX lists, she'd looked up the material on Virtech that *Technology Week* had on file. The two orders had been delayed. Virtech would have had cash flow problems. It seems that it hadn't gone to a bank but to a large private investor to solve those problems. It had sold equity for an injection of cash. The paper had run a couple of lines on it a month or so ago. The name of the investor was MT Industries Holdings. Nothing sinister about that, except the connection that Warren had provided for her. MT Industries had a licence to handle credit, to be a credit card company.

'Now, Warren told me that at his level of the game, you had to use the game's own credit card. You put up so much stake money and get a number. It credits you if you win and direct debits your bank account if you go over. Gets interest, et cetera, just like my Harvey Nichols account,' she said, and I wondered who'd be paying for that one day. 'She's bankrolling him. If JJ 1000 is her, then Pornoland is too. If it's her game, so is the credit card company. She's the banker, so it must be. And if she is, then she actually owns a big chunk of Virtech. Power behind the throne. MT Industries is the link between that game and Virtech. What do you think?'

She looked very pleased with herself. Well she might. I hadn't got that far but then, I had had other distractions and I hadn't slept with Warren. I didn't jump to her conclusions either.

'There's something else, George, Warren saw something there in the VR machine. I didn't get a look in with that Jones guy but he seemed to know Warren. He invited him to play some sort of VR game. It was all very polite just as if the chaps were retiring for port and cigars, you know. But when Warren came out, well, he was really mad. He hit the guy really hard, I thought he was going to kill him. I managed to get him off and into the car but he kept yelling about giving you the hiding he should have given you years ago. Heap big macho deal.'

'What else did he say about me?'

'Not a good word, I'm afraid. He dumped me at home and took off. I called right away, but you weren't in.'

'You didn't call the police?'

'No. Did he hurt you?'

'No. Get me a Scotch, will you?'

'George, it's nearly breakfast . . .'

I gave her a look that made her do as I'd asked. She shuffled out of the door in Richard's leather mules and I rose from my chair to put my cup on the drainer. I didn't bother to wash up. My head was buzzing. I could see David's face at the back of my mind, could hear him whispering. Reusable. Like a glass. Fill it up. Empty it. Start all over again. See? The clink of a heavy tumbler startled me and I turned. Diane was standing beside me.

'Do you want to talk?' she said.

'Not now,' I said and she patted my shoulder.

'OK, but I'm starting on what I've got today. Julie Jones has got a lot of explaining to do,' she said, and I thought, good luck.

I couldn't sleep. I lay on my bed, bleached, burned and battered. I wanted so much to be different from what David had wanted but it didn't really matter. I had been deconstructed and pieced together in some computer program. Diane and Richard were making up again in the bedroom next door. Mr and Mrs Jones were probably doing the same in theirs, wrapped in clingfilm and Brillo pads or something good and weird. Warren was floating in the half-life of a coma and that left me. And Max.

Max.

I leaped off the bed. I was never going to sleep with this on my mind and there was only one other person I knew who was a paid-up member of Insomniacs Abroad. Max Winters. No one ever saw him wheel himself up to his desk at *Technology Week* or ever saw him leave. He sat with his useless legs tucked under the machine that transported him to the big outside. He accessed databases and friends with access to databases, all over the world. It was no time at all for him to be working.

The telephone rang for a long while.

'Yes.' It was Max.

'Max, it's me, Georgina Powers.'

'Yes.'

'I need a fix on MT Industries Holdings.'

'For the story you're working on for *Technology Week*?'

'Yes.'

'I presume we'll be getting this one first this time, since we appear to be providing the resources.'

'Naturally.'

I heard him sucking in the smoke from his cigar. 'Are you in today?' he said.

'I have to visit a sick friend. Can you call me back?'

He cut me off. Manners, Mr Winters. Manners.

I'd been asleep for about two hours when the phone rang. I rolled quickly out of bed to get to it before either of the lovebirds breakfasting in the kitchen could. My reflection in the mirror startled me. I looked like an Australian lifeguard waiting for his Charles Atlas course to slide through the letter box. But I looked good. What I lacked in muscle definition, I gained through skin tone. It was incredible how healthy a tan can make you look even if you feel like you've just had brain surgery.

I croaked into the mouthpiece of the handset and Max began to speak.

'MT Industries Holdings is a private company registered in the Cayman Islands. However, other MT Industries companies pop up in Rio, California, Florida and Nevada with interests in property, finance, entertainment and leisure rather than manufacturing. I wonder if MT is the operative word. Oh yes, recently bailed out Virtech.'

I thanked him and replaced the receiver. MT. Empty. Whose idea of a joke was that? His? Hers?

Wait a minute. Nevada? Las Vegas was in Nevada and Warren worked in Las Vegas. Now, I don't believe in coincidences and this was one I definitely wanted cleared up. Unfortunately, the man who could help me most was in no position to tell me anything. No harm in jogging his memory though. It might help him wake up.

It wasn't visiting time but the sister let me in to see him. His appearance made me forget what I'd come for.

He hadn't regained consciousness since the ambulance had brought him in the night before. They'd checked out his central nervous system, which seemed to be working, but he still hadn't come round. The sister said that if he didn't come to in twenty-four hours, they'd start to worry, but she fully expected him to regain consciousness before then.

A tube sprouted from between his ribs and twisted down the side of the bed into a water bottle.

'Quite a few ribs broken. One punctured his lung so we've fixed up an underwater seal to clear the air out. We're happy with his breathing though. No ventilator, you notice,' she said.

I nodded and looked at Warren's tenderized face. The road, or an overpriced trainer, had taken the skin from his cheeks and nose. Bandages held his chin up to the rest of his head and both swollen eyelids were as purple and shiny smooth as ripe aubergines. His bulbous top lip hung idiotically over the bottom as if he was trying to remember something. He was stable, she said, thank God.

'Thank you,' I said, tears in my eyes.

We stood at the end of the bed and the sister whispered as if she was trying not to wake him. 'Does he have any family?'

I shrugged.

I had never met Warren's family. He hadn't exactly taken me home to mother and all I could remember of her was that she had lived off the Romford Road in Forest Gate. I didn't know if she did now, what with all that money he'd taken. Maybe he'd set her up some-where. Maybe she lived in Las Vegas, if anyone did. I thought the place was just full of hotels and staff quarters. The Dice Palace. He worked there. They might know. I could get its number and call.

We both turned at the sound of the door opening and a policeman popped his head round. The sister stepped outside, leaving me alone with Warren's bloated face and broken body. I felt ashamed. Ashamed for the men who'd bludgeoned him senseless, just for driving a big car with a blonde white girl by his side. Ashamed at myself for not defending him, for having him defend me like he had always wanted to. Warren was an old-fashioned East End boy. For him, women were for pedestals or purgatory and, no matter what, I was the former, a ragamuffin queen for the ragamuffin boy.

'Warren, wake up, Warren, please,' I said.

The reply was a rasping snore as his breath laboured through his blood-crusted nose and mouth.

That's all I could think of to say. I've seen films of people sitting by bedsides chatting to bodies whose occupants had metaphorical suitcases in both hands and had all but caught the last train. I couldn't do that, talk and not hear answers. I couldn't just speak my thoughts. I needed reactions, even from myself. I stood by the side of the complicated steel bed and stared at his head, wrapped up and lying heavy on the pillow, his brown arms straight by his side, veins punctured and taped, sucking in the saline that dripped from a bottle on a high chrome stand. A discreet tube took urine from under the white labelled sheet to a discreet plastic container below. His helplessness was complete and all I could do was stare. I stood there for a while until I had almost convinced myself that he was pretending, that he knew I was standing there watching him, taking in the detail of his body, and that if I turned to walk away, he'd call my name.

'Warren?' I said.

Nothing. Not a flicker, just that gasping sound of his

breath squeezing in and out of his damaged system. I listened and watched until I found I wasn't thinking about him but about the nature of sympathy. I wondered if it was linked to notions of dominance. My mind wandered through examples of puppies turning their tails to bigger dogs, of appeasement rituals that all made the potential aggressor appear stronger and safer. I wondered if women became nurses, not because of some desire to help the sick but through some desire to feel strong, and on and on until Warren may as well have been alone in the room for all the good I was doing him.

It was his leg sticking out from under the sheet that drew my attention back to the patient. My thoughts popped away all at once. It had very little hair and scarcely a mark except for one small, ancient scar under the bony knee. Disembodied from its bludgeoned torso, it appeared to be in marvellous, sinewy shape. It was the sort of leg that you would want to see in stretch cycling shorts the colour of bubble gum, or dark Lycra tights and soft dancing shoes. Its long brown foot, with gently curving arch, stretched out into long elegant toes evenly decorated with pearly clean-cut nails. Its pinkish brown sole was smooth and uncalloused.

I wanted to put my hand on the shin and push along the coffee-coloured skin up to the thigh. Looking quickly at Warren's face to check that he was really sleeping, I stretched out my hand to touch him, took my fingers back and then reached out again. His skin was warm. I had stood there watching the tubes and pipes, forgetting that he was still alive, warm and alive, fighting deep down to get back. My fingers curled around the bone and muscle and squeezed. I stroked his skin in silence until the door swished open and the sister called to me.

I stood up and looked down at Warren. 'Don't go away now,' I said.

*

The policeman took me to the station. His sergeant wanted me to look through Warren's luggage, see if I could help them. I didn't know then that his name had come up on the police national computer and no information could be had unless the policeman asking put his name, rank and number into the machine first.

'Who wants to know?' the computer had said, like any street hood. Naturally enough, the boys on the case wanted to check him out a little before they committed themselves.

'You're sure this mob were not known to Mr Graham?' the sergeant said, unzipping Warren's soft leather suitcase.

'I'm sure,' I replied.

Warren's baseball cap with the roulette wheel design lay on top of his clothes. There was a black towelling bathrobe and no pyjamas that we could see, another pair of Levi 501s, some T-shirts, two cotton shirts by Paul Smith and one blue and red silk tie. There was a bag for his toiletries, one pair of Gucci moccasins and, unbelievably, a pair of ornate cowboy boots. There was a suit bag, too, with a smooth number by Armani folded inside. The sergeant raised an eyebrow.

'Security, you say. Pays well, does it, in America?'

'He's a single man,' I said, remembering the missing weapon. The sergeant nodded and tucked his hand into the deep pockets of the bag. He pulled out an old photo booth strip of colour photographs. They were of Warren and me pulling stupid faces at the camera. He'd had a short mane of dreads in those days and a really happy smile. So had I. A naughty young grin. In one shot, I'd put two fingers up behind his head. What a sense of humour.

I smiled at the policeman and shrugged my shoulders. 'Happy days.'

'You?' said the sergeant, tapping the two-finger shot.

'I don't think that was my natural colour either,' I said, as the sergeant held them up to my face and put them down.

'Ah,' he said, feeling down into the bag again like a surgeon probing for something untoward in a warm body cavity. He pulled out a thin collection of business cards. There was Warren's name. Warren S. Graham. S? I didn't know there was an S. After that came Proprietor, The Dice Palace, Las Vegas, Nevada, a zipcode, a telephone number and, tucked in the corner of the card, a couple of black and red dice.

'His passport says businessman,' said the sergeant.

'Well, it's not far from the truth,' I said, beginning to feel uneasy with the sergeant feeling his way around.

'You said security. Computer security.'

'That's what he told me.'

The sergeant tapped the card against his hand. 'You didn't know he owned this place?'

'I didn't know he'd done that well.'

'He's on our computer. That means he has form, Miss Powers.'

'Mrs. It's Mrs Powers.'

The dancing eyebrows lifted again.

'I'm divorced. Warren's just a friend over here on holiday.'

'I see. He's a friend, who doesn't tell you what he does, checks out of the Savoy but doesn't leave town, gets beaten up somewhere in the East End and turns up on the PNC. How so, Mrs Powers? How so?'

'Look, he's not a criminal or anything. If that's his place, he would be involved with the computers. He's good with computers, brilliant in fact. What did his records say?'

'Why didn't he tell you he owned the place?'

'Maybe he just wanted to surprise me. Came back here to take me off into the sunset, you know how it is.'

'Well, in that case, this will interest you even more, Mrs Powers.' He emphasized the Mrs with unnecessary satisfaction and, holding the passport, pointed down at the first page. 'Here, under marital status.'

The sergeant handed the book to me. I looked at Warren's crim shot photo and down to the line the sergeant wanted me to read.

It said: Married.

'Don't you think you should let her know about this,' I said, handing the book back. The sergeant nodded, smiled and told me it was OK to leave.

The colour of envy is green and black, striped like a cat's back, strung tight like a bow. It tangoed away in my tightening chest, spun around like a dancer and arched over me, tap-tapping its feet like hammers on a drum. I had tried to be cute with the nice police officer but he had already read the lines. Warren had a wife, and I didn't want her to exist. I didn't like the idea of someone else intruding into the turbulent airspace we shared. I stood on the pavement, the traffic and the late summer wind whirling sweet wrappings up and round my pinky-brown legs. I took the half-smoked cigarette out of my mouth and crushed it under my black-sandalled heel. The man hadn't changed. He never had placed both hands flat on the table between us so that I could see. Instead, he caressed me with one and held the other behind his back, fingers crossed. I'd been suckered, again, but for what this time? A big red bus came before a black cab, and I jumped on. I was going to miss visiting hours for the rest of the week.

I went back home and sat at my desk, thinking. MT Industries Holdings had invested in Virtech. According to Diane, on information from Warren, it was also running a credit card company that provided facilities for Julie Jones's Pornoland and its gambling business. Diane reckoned that Julie was the banker, that she was MT

161

Industries. I wasn't so sure. Diane hadn't had time to check it out, to find out that MT Industries had a subsidiary in Nevada. Las Vegas was in Nevada, as was Warren's Dice Palace. These places had to register their accounts just like any other company, and if that was so it would be on a database somewhere. I didn't want to trouble Max again with the request to check out a casino, so I looked at the card in my hand and checked the time – 2.30 p.m. Another couple of hours and I could give them a call. I didn't want to catch them between shifts.

My thoughts ticked through my mind like wall-clocks in a jeweller's shop. The sash window in my room was open at the bottom and a gentle breeze blew in past the curtains. Who would I ask for? Mrs Graham, the proprietor's wife? Would I be nice or icy? Nice was for nobodies; I wanted to be as cruel as a steel needle. Hi, I'm the one who turned him down the first time he asked. Don't expect him, honey, he might be dead in a week. Oh yes, there's something else. I had the last, good kiss.

I muttered to myself, glad to get it off my chest because I knew I'd say none of it when faced with a real voice. My eyes felt heavy. It was time for a break. I set my calculator alarm because I wasn't sure that I'd be awake for the next two minutes, never mind hours, but, as I climbed on to the bed, the telephone rang.

It was David.

'The best way to kill a dog is to cut off his head,' he said, without introducing himself. He sounded as if he had a cold. Maybe Warren had broken his nose.

'Confucius?' I replied.

'John Patterson.'

'*The* John Patterson or the guy who's marketing manager for . . .'

'*The*.'

I had to think what he meant. Then it came home. John Patterson ran National Cash Register at the start of this century. He was famous for two things: doing almost anything, short of murder, to monopolize a market, and teaching Thomas J. Watson of IBM how to do it too. It was more than dog eat dog in their world, more than survival of the fittest. It was survival of the one with the big chopper, and yes, I mean that both ways.

'Why are you telling me this, David?' I said.

'I'm telling you about the nature of competition and the nature of winning.'

'Competing for what, winning what?'

'People.'

'I still don't understand.'

'The black man won't win. I will.'

'You lost a long time ago and the so-called black man was never in the race.'

'He thinks he is, and so do I.'

'Well, you're both well out of it now, so cut the Hammer horrors crap. I saw your wife yesterday. Did she tell you? No? Did she tell you we had a ride in your machine? She tell you that I know about the little disks, about Pornoland too?'

He didn't speak. The silence lengthened until I had to ask if he was still there.

'What are you talking about?' he said.

'The digitized videos of Julie's blow job, of your snuff movie, of me with a different body gyrating for punters who win me in the game.'

'What game?'

'David, I know, so don't jerk me around. She said you made her video us at IPEX. You sent her to me. Warren, the black man, remember? He won me in a computer game, in Pornoland, the one she runs through JJ 1000. That's why he came. He won me.'

'She did that?'

'Yes.'

'She knows who you are?' he said.

163

'Yes, she always has, and one more thing, check out MT Industries. Either she owns you or the black man does. I've yet to check that one out. Great story, thanks.'

He didn't answer. He'd gone.

I said to hell with him and lay down to sleep, my heart pumping. I breathed deeply four or five times and tried to relax.

The calculator's monotonous beep woke me. It had tried to rouse me for at least ten minutes. That's the real beauty of microchips, persistence and indifference.

I stumbled to the bathroom to flannel my face, and, only slightly more alert, went to the kitchen to make a mug of strong instant coffee. Back in my room, I tapped out 0101 and the number for The Dice Palace. The receptionist told me that Mr Graham was on holiday in England and asked if I was from there too and was it cold and did it rain all the time like Mr Graham said. I told her that I was, that it didn't, that this was an expensive call and that I needed to speak to whoever was in charge, soon.

'That'll be Mr Powers,' she said. 'And who is calling?'

I rested my forehead on the hard palm of my hand. It couldn't be.

'Mrs Powers,' I said.

'Georgina, is that you?' said an all-American voice.

'Hello, Eddie,' I said, shaking open a worryingly light packet of cigarettes. There was one left and all was well with the world.

CHAPTER FOURTEEN

Eddie, my ex-husband, sounded pleased and surprised to hear from me. I was surprised, too. I thought he ran a software company in Southern California. I didn't think he and Warren, who'd never been close personal friends, would be working together. The last time they did they both got in, and out of, a lot of trouble. He wanted to shoot the breeze, as he liked to say, but I got right to the point. I told him that Warren had been beaten up and that he was lying comatose in hospital.

'Shit,' Eddie said. It could have been a statement of sympathy or irritation, but I couldn't work out which.

'So can you tell his wife?' I said.

'His wife?'

'His passport gives his marital status as married.'

'Oh.'

'Never mind. I've got a card here that says he's the proprietor of The Dice Palace, is that right?'

'That's right. Hey, did you two fall out?'

'We all fell out, remember?'

He said that he did, but that he didn't think I'd still be such a pain in the ass about it. We were building up for a row and I didn't want that, not long distance and not when I was picking up the bill. I asked about Warren's mother.

'She died. New Year's Day.'

'Any other family?'

'Well, apart from this so-called wife you tell me about, no one. Tell me now, is he real sick?'

'He could die, Eddie.'

The words stuck in my throat with an undelivered sob. I had to pull myself together. Eddie was the last person I wanted to hear me cry. Correction, the last but one. Warren was the last person. I didn't want to cry on my time either and though I'd never had him down as telepathic, Eddie told me to put down the phone and he'd call me back. By the time I'd wiped my eyes and blown my nose, the telephone was ringing.

'I want to know why he came here. Wasn't he taking a risk, with the authorities?'

'You mean the other business? That's all taken care of. It's cool. We all did a deal, remember? All we have to do is keep nice and clean ... and quiet.' The patter of Eddie's brain cells synchronizing echoed down the line. 'Hey, you don't think anyone else got to him?'

'No, I don't think. It was out of the blue. I'm sure of that.'

'How sure?'

'Not that sure of anything. Why did he come, Eddie?'

'For you. He said he had to see you. Didn't he tell you?'

'Sort of, but you know Warren. When has he ever played it straight with me?'

'It's hard for him.'

'Hard for me too.'

'Georgina. Me too. But, we tried and, well, I got no hold on you. I got my own life now, you know? You too, huh? But Warren ... he's like the fucking IRS. He never forgets. You were the one for him. Period.'

'Bullshit.'

'OK. He got up one day, nice bright morning, 'cos that's all we have round here, and said, "I'm off to get

166

George." That was it. For what it's worth, I told him, don't hold your breath, mate.'

'He carry a gun that you know?'

'What?'

'You don't know anything else? You don't know about any game?'

'What game's that, George?' His voice came down low and easy, relaxed. The gun had come as a real surprise, but this, this hadn't.

'Thing called Pornoland. It's a game for gamblers with dirty minds and twitchy dicks.'

'This a story, that what you're on to? No. I don't know. And I wouldn't want anyone to hear that we do. We have a licence to protect here.'

'He said something about MT Industries and a credit card company,' I said.

'He did? Well, yeah, that's us. You know how it is, we had to do something with the nickels and dimes.' He laughed and said, 'Hi fellas,' down the phone as if he thought someone might be listening.

I hung on in silence until he said, 'Where is he?'

'The London.'

'Is he real sick?'

'I told you. He's sick, Eddie.'

'But he ain't dead yet?'

'No.'

'In that case, I have to take care of business, George. You keep in touch now.'

With that, he cleared the line.

My ex-husband Eddie was a crook. He hadn't always been but he had always had the potential. When temptation shimmered in seven to eight figure numbers, he didn't think twice. He closed the circuit. Warren was the same. I'd like to think I would have turned it down but then I was never given the choice. I could only handle the petty stuff, like expenses, which at Max's had

struggled to run into double figures, never mind temptation.

The real trouble with Eddie was not that he was bad,
but that he could not be trusted. He'd betrayed me with
my best friend, though I couldn't damn him for that now,
not with my current record. The fact was, he was a
natural liar and cheat. It was the only way he knew to
keep everybody happy. He was tall, dark, and handsome
too, very good with his hands, if you know what I mean,
and dangerously plausible. If there was a law against
impersonating a good guy, Eddie would be serving time.

Warren had never been taken in by Eddie. He wasn't
susceptible to that sort of charm, I suppose. They did
have interests in common, though. One was money and
the other was the nurture of a single figure. They looked
after Number One. So the fact that they were working
together in a casino in Vegas had to be to a mutual
advantage and not just for old times' sake. With the tidy
little company in the Caymans taking the strain of all
their investments, everything must have been hunky dory,
until I made my presence felt like a forgotten clamp in an
otherwise perfectly stitched-up operation.

Diane had got it wrong. It wasn't Julie Jones who was
bailing out Virtech, it was MT Industries Holdings, Eddie
and Warren. If Eddie was telling the truth, then Warren
had more than a player's interest in Pornoland, he had
money in it. I clenched my fists and shook them. I knew
he had been up to something. I knew it. He must have
come back to check things out, find out why I'd turned
up in his game, and what sort of trouble that might
mean.

Julie Jones had to know who MT Industries really was,
and if David didn't, then I had given him a clue. I tried to
think back to when Julie had met Warren. They hadn't
known each other then, at least they made it seem that
way. She knew that I wasn't Cabbie, though. She was a

168

clever woman. She must have guessed that it was him in the bar. I had told her that he'd played the game and he'd reminisced about his life driving around the London streets. Eddie must have confirmed it by now. I bet he picked up the phone and called her the moment he'd finished with me. How did she stop laughing out loud when I started to talk about credit card numbers and quarters of a million? Damn her. Damn Eddie. Damn Warren. Damn the one niggling little question mark. Why had he run up a bill for a quarter of a million on his own game and then wiped his tracks? I wanted to ask him so many questions now, and 'How are you? Do you think you'll live?' were way down the list.

The telephone rang again.

'Mrs Powers?' It was my friend in the force, Robert Falk. He liked the formality of calling me Mrs Powers, and liked me to call him Robert. In our civilized stand-offish relationship, we were never Bob and George. We had leisurely dinners out together and sometimes he'd take me to a fight. He thought I didn't understand the sport of boxing and how working class heroes are made. He had theories on both, which lasted well past a six pack or a single bottle of wine. I thought he was lonely, and he thought I was. We were good friends.

'Anything to tell me, Mrs Powers?' His voice had dropped an octave. He was teasing me like an old-fashioned uncle would a boy with his pockets stuffed with stolen apples.

'Warren Graham's been around. He's in the London,' I said.

'Very poorly too, so I understand.'

'Yes.'

'Any idea what business he had here?'

'He came to see me.'

'About what, exactly?'

'Personal business.'

'Nothing to do with MT Industries Holdings then?'

'You know about that?'

'Mrs Powers, I have a very impressive file on Warren S. Graham, for information only, you understand. We have to ensure he keeps his side of the bargain.'

'Hands above blankets.'

'Where we can see them. We keep track of his contacts over here. The FBI keeps track of them over there. A hacker like that can't be allowed to go underground again. Always dangerous, but potentially useful, you know.'

I was beginning to feel uncomfortable talking to my friend Robert. He had no more accepted that Warren and Eddie had walked away, rich and free down the yellow brick road, than I had. Pornoland would not have been something MT Industries could be involved in and I wanted to find out a bit more before I dropped Warren in it with his minders. Falk was all but asking me, so he couldn't know about the game, or he'd have jumped at it.

'Did you know he and Eddie were working together?' I said.

'Yes. Curious relationship, for Mr Graham.'

'Why didn't you tell me?'

'You always seem to have enough problems of your own without my adding to them.'

'I resent that,' I said.

'You didn't know this mob that hit Graham the other night?'

'No. They were NF types. Took exception to the car and me.'

'The blonde.'

'Are you laughing at me, Robert?'

'No, but this I have to see.'

He knew I was on to something because he told me one thing that was going to ensure that I lost another night's sleep. Eddie had made the deal with Virtech. Eddie, the white all-American male, made all the deals for MT Industries and Warren, the coffee-coloured no-man's man, hid away and signed them. David had met Eddie before, but not Warren. Maybe Julie had only ever met Eddie, too, and she thought Cabbie – Warren – was a real punter. She didn't know who he really was. Her banker. I said it was interesting, and Robert said one more thing. He asked me if the program I'd sent him had anything to do with any of this. As he recalled, the gentleman involved looked remarkably similar to one Dr David Jones, founder of Virtech.

I told him half of it, about me and Mrs Jones and her warped idea of revenge. I mentioned two disks, not three, and left out the bit about her husband's death fantasies. There was no need to over-egg the pudding.

'What you need, Mrs Powers, is a holiday,' he said.

'That's what Warren suggested.'

'With him?'

'Yes. He's a trier, isn't he?'

Warren was still unconscious. It was almost up to the wire and nothing had changed. Twenty-four hours and then they start to worry. I nodded at the nurses and went straight in to him. He lay there naked but for bandages that ravelled round his chest, and head. The drip above his head silently pumped fluid into a vein and the other below the bed took it out. The tube from his chest bubbled misplaced air from his lungs safely underwater.

His lips were fixed half open, cracking dry and white, and his curly-lashed eyes closed on nothing, not even dreams. Sitting by his bed, I resisted the urge to shake him awake. I wanted to know why he had to lead me such a dance. I wanted to tell him how confused I was. Was he my friend, or wasn't he? I had things to say and as I spoke, I took his hand which was as dry as an autumn leaf. I spoke with some difficulty at first, but once I had started and gone a little way, it was easy. I told him about Eddie and how strange it was that the two of them were together, partners in crime, once again. I asked him why he had to come such a long way to lie to me. I asked what he owed Julie Jones apart from £250,000 of their own money. I asked him about his wife and if she was pretty. I asked if they'd been married long and if they had kids. I told him how jealous I was. I fiddled with his fingernails and told him things I would never have told him to his conscious face. I told him that I loved him, and hated him, and all that stuff. He didn't twitch so much as an eyelid and after half an hour I left, relieved that no one knew the truth now, but me.

The sister spoke as I passed the desk.

'You look upset. Was he asleep again?'

I stopped and turned to her. 'Asleep again?'

'He regained consciousness three hours ago. He'll be fine now, don't you worry.'

I pushed through the swing doors and hurried down the mushroom-coloured corridor with its odour of laundered sheets and disinfected wounds. Why should I worry? I'd just go back and shoot the bastard.

The cab ticked over outside the house. It was late but the light that was on in the lounge helped me see into my handbag for keys and money. I was a little unsteady on my feet. After my visit to the hospital, I had decided to visit a couple of bars and work my way through a few bowls of peanuts. It had given me time to think.

I couldn't expose MT Industries for anything more than being a credit card company and major investor in a high tech firm. Computerized credit card accounts were just numbers – so much virtual cash. I couldn't hope to prove that the flow of any of it had been as a result of a pornographic gambling game. I only knew one punter who was involved, Warren. Hardly a star witness, and his friend, Eddie, would have done the necessary house-keeping by now.

I did have screen prints of the game that would prove it had existed. I had the telephone number of JJ 1000 and the telephone number of Pornoland. I could ring around, see if anyone had played on JJ 1000. I could ask if anyone had heard of Pornoland. Someone might have. My credit card account would have been credited with my winnings by now, if Julie Jones hadn't cancelled the whole day's play when she pulled the plug. If she hadn't, my credit card company would tell me who had credited my account. I had the disk of myself which wasn't much use, because it could have come from anywhere, unless I was prepared to show the others and say they came from her. I'd link her name with David's, describe the project at Virtech – that's when I'd bring in MT Industries; I'd emphasize the potential of virtual porn. I had enough for the perfect story, no politicians, peers or priests, but it had plenty of sex and money, still a high-scoring combination in any circulation war.

The cab pulled away and I stood by the park railings breathing in the air. It was cooler than it had been and the night was dark. Summer was coming to an end and I was going to take Robert Falk's advice and go on holiday after I'd finished this business. I was going to get away from all of them, get a real suntan on some foreign beach, all by myself. The television was flickering in the lounge and I assumed that Diane and Richard would be cosying up together on the sofa. Venus and Hephaestus. She had the story too, but she didn't have as much as me. I was going to do this one without her, I thought, swaying by the kerb. She had no right to it. I'd lived it, and she'd stolen it. Let her be lucky in love. Let me have the by-line.

Someone's face appeared at the window. A fair-haired, bespectacled head looked down at me. He must have cut a set of my keys. There was no tingling thrill this time. I could hardly move for the heavy disappointment I felt at the sight of him. It wasn't that I was too drunk to feel fear. After the initial twist in the gut, I was, simply, irritated. I'd have to tell him that he had cured at least one person with covert behavioural therapy, and all the patient wanted to do was go to her room, fall on her face and sleep for a week. His face disappeared from the window and I studied the line of parked cars and neighbouring houses. There were lights on all along the street, curtains drawn and some not. It wasn't late, people were still awake. I wasn't alone, I could run to any door. But when my door opened, I turned and hurried away. He'd cut me off, left me stranded on the other side of the empty street where the thick clusters of trees and little night animals were. I heard the click of his leather shoes down the steps and on to the pavement. My feet doubled the pace, broke into a fast walk, then a run but it didn't help. I could hear the feet tick-tacking behind me. My satchel bag swung off one shoulder and hit the ground like a boulder, the strap winding tight around my ankle. I stumbled forward, and scorching the palms of my hands along the concrete did not prevent my forehead connecting with the kerb.

I remember leaning on him, walking too quickly together, his arm around me, his strong hand under my arm. He was talking quietly to me, encouraging me but I just couldn't make the steps.

'Georgina.'

It was David whispering in the dark.

'Not now, David. Fer Chrissakes,' I muttered.

'Georgina, I'm afraid.'

I remembered right away, swung my hand over to switch on the sidelight. I blinked up at him, blinked again. My head hurt. I was naked and so was he. I looked down at myself and then at him. It had happened without my consent. I smiled sickly and let my head sink back into my pillow. Without consent. No point in screaming now, I thought. My unconsciousness had served his purpose and had probably saved my life. Let no one ever lecture me on the evils of drink. I'd remind them that David was always sober. I was going to have to keep him talking. I could talk to him, up to a point.

'Did you have a nice time?' I said.

'It was OK.'

'Just OK?'

'Your hair. Your skin. It isn't the same.'

'You don't like it?'

'Not as much.'

'What are you afraid of, the dark?' I said.

'I'm afraid of her.'

'Why?'

'She loved me.'

'I know. She risked a fortune and her own reputation to make me look a fool. Why should that make you afraid?'

'I told you before, it's too dangerous.'

'I don't understand.'

'Love lets people in. They can destroy you. You don't love me. I don't love you. We fit, though. That's perfect.'

'I spoke to her. She wants to hurt me, not you.'

'You don't understand. I made her be you.'

'What do you mean?'

'In the machine. It was all right until she found out who you really were. I didn't know she knew.'

I began to feel some sympathy for Julie Jones. It takes a real bastard to dress his wife up so he can fantasize about his mistress. He had humiliated her. She'd offered herself to be his whim, and he had betrayed her, without leaving the room. Without consent. Without consent. God, why couldn't he leave me alone?

'I thought you'd had affairs before,' I said.

'I did. It was all one way. I could be for them, but never be myself. It was a relief to return to her.'

'She told me you made her video me and make those disks.'

'I didn't. No. She did it to make a fool of me. I should never have given her the right to know me. She broke the rules.'

'I thought you did.'

'No.'

I turned my back to him and leaned over the bed to look for my handbag and a cigarette. My swollen head felt as if it might drop on to the carpet and roll under the wardrobe. Their relationship was as complex and fragile as the mating dance of two poisonous spiders: one false move and it was suppertime. I took a long drag of what I suppose was a postprandial cigarette. He had lapsed into silence, staring out across the humps and bumps of my duvet. I leaned on one elbow, resting my head in my hand, gazing at his fuzzy half-lit image beside me. He had a bruise on his cheek just under the eye, and his nose was swollen. Without his spectacles, his blue myopic eyes gave him an air of vulnerability, and that's what he was, vulnerable, to all the things that I was protected from. He had had to build himself a defence – callousness that protected him, like industrial glasses protected the moist, exposed tissue of the human eye from darting shards of hot metal.

'Can't you trust anyone, David?' I said.

'I trust you.'

'For God's sake, why?'

'We fit. You don't understand yet how we fit. Julie understands, that's why I'm afraid. I was wrong to show her. I made a mistake letting her in.'

'Show her what?'

'Myself.'

I waited before speaking again. She was crazy. He was crazy. He thought he was in danger, but in how much danger was I? I was hardly her best buddy. That was threat number one, short term. He had more than revealed himself to me: he found that a threat to himself. That was threat number two, long term. I flicked ash nonchalantly into an old tinfoil dish by my bedside and wished I knew the name of his doctor.

'Tell me, David, this machine you've got, the one with us in it, how's it working?' I said.

'Strange, you work in virtual reality and you start to appreciate reality more, the natural complexity of it. I see you in there, as I created you, a software trick, with polygons and vector graphics simulating form and motion. Too simple. With you tonight I could feel the material structure, the organics, as if I were pulling you apart and putting you together, not just as human flesh but as a part of the universe, as atoms, molecules, matter. I never know how I'm going to feel. It's more . . . more spontaneous. It would have been perfect, if you'd looked the same.'

That was it. I pushed back the covers and swung my legs over the side of the bed, almost collapsing backwards immediately with pain. I didn't like to suggest that while the noble savage was recreating me, he could have disconnected the pain centres in my head. I pressed my hands hard down on to the bed and lifted myself up. He watched me as I distanced myself from him, walking naked, past the mirror, lightly tanned except for little stripes of bikini white. The weekend in the sun hadn't worked. His wife was right. Eroticism is in the mind. It was the sickly features I had had a week ago that unleashed his imagination. He said it wasn't the same, me being blonde and brown, but that hadn't stopped him playing God again. I didn't have to be there but it helped, an awful lot, especially when he didn't have to take no for an answer.

I slipped into my clothes trying to look casual and relaxed. My right leg trembled a little and it took real effort to keep the shaking from my voice. She could have him, slice him, wrap him in hot foil, whatever the two of them liked to do most, so long as he got the hell out of my life.

I tried to sound reasonable and not whine when I spoke. 'David, we could have met somewhere else. Why did you come here tonight? Richard and Diane, they could have been here, you know.' It sounded like, Honey, the children could have walked in on us.

His fingers twitched together, snapping imaginary matchsticks, and his tongue moved around the inside of his lips as if it were a round sweet. I watched him as he threw the covers back and began to dress too.

When he spoke, he sounded satisfied, happy. What he told me was as comforting as a blue blanket stitched with razor blades.

'I had to save myself, that's all, save you for me, and save myself. Don't worry, it's going to be all right now,' he said, zipping his fly. 'You know, the irony is that tonight she would have been perfect.'

He smiled, like a man who has seen the morning sun peek through the windows and promise a perfect day. He didn't touch me again. He made himself a drink in the kitchen and then left.

CHAPTER FIFTEEN

Julie Jones's death blew the virtual sex story right out into the open. It carried Diane's by-line in *Technology Week*, and mine in the nationals because Robert Falk heard about it and gave it to me first. Diane had to work her cute little butt off following it up.

None of the facts presented at the inquest, six weeks later, proved foul play. The police had kept an open mind on the possibility of suicide but the coroner was having none of it. Julie Jones had left no notes, scrawled in her own hand, or tapped into her personal computer, that would explain why she had felt depressed enough to take her own life. No one who knew her or worked with her could say that she had been other than her normal self, whatever that was, for it came as a great surprise to all that she was a frequent user of the sex machine.

Her immediate family did not attend the inquest. Perhaps they did not want to hear that their shining, successful girl died sheathed in a wired suit connected to a computer. The cause of death was strangulation, and it was no fake vision from a frame grab, no harmless sexual exercise in a fabricated universe, no pretend squeezing on a hotel bed. This was the real thing: choking, gasping, burning for breath, thrashing with pain, and a permanent stain of nasty little welts.

The computer's force-feedback mechanism had failed, or rather worked too well. The pockets of air in the fabric of the suit had inflated beyond their parameters, pressing in and around her throat, tightening until she couldn't take in any air at all. The reality of death had grown out of a computer dream, like a mushroom in a fairy circle, overnight.

The police had questioned David, and me, but our secrets had not been revealed. We were having an affair, that's all. We'd been miles away and she had been alone. The suit had not been faulty. It had not been tampered with. The hardware and the software had behaved normally. The system had been designed to tolerate extreme requirements and the computer sent and received instructions from the virtual world and the suit's sensors. It was up to the user to set the desired parameters and there was no question that, as an experienced user, Julie Jones would have done so.

Warren had read about it in the papers and seen it on the television. With all the furore, I hadn't managed to see him for nearly a week and he was less than understanding.

'After all that happened between you and him, you and me, you sleep with this fuck?' he said, holding his chest. They'd taken out the tube and left a stitch in his side, but his ribs, which were still mending, were sore. The row we were having was not helping.

'I told you what I told them. I didn't sleep with him. I'd had a few drinks but I hit my head running away. When I came to, there we were.'

Warren pulled a simpering face and mimicked me. 'It was all a dream, officer. Oh, gimme a break. What you think this is, fucking Dallas?'

'I came here. I left. I had a few drinks. I went home and there he was. I hit my head running away from him. It's the truth.'

'Oh yeah? How come you didn't scream the fucking place down when you woke up to find him snuggling up?

Why didn't you tell the old Bill he scared you shitless, he liked to put his hands round your throat and squeeze hard, like he did to her?'

'Don't you think it was bad enough that he was with me when she died, for Chrissakes! If he killed his wife, he didn't do it with his bare hands. I don't know what he did with his hands. He raped me, Warren. I couldn't tell anyone. He did. He raped me.'

'You love it, don't you? His sick stuff.'

'Oh, thanks.'

'You gonna cover up for him?'

'Look, no one knows what happened. Nothing was done to that suit or that computer that she couldn't have done herself, or could have happened accidentally. She should have checked the suit.'

'Did you? I fucking didn't,' he said.

Our voices filled the room as Warren hobbled around it, looking for space to put all his rage and frustration. When he turned to me his eyes were squeezed shut. 'He set her up, you stupid bitch. He set her up.'

The shouting made him cough and splutter but when I ran over to support him, he pushed me away.

'Jesus, anyone'd think I killed her,' I said, letting go of his arm.

'You helped.'

I went to slap his already battered face and he caught my arm. We faced each other, breathing hard like bare-knuckled fighters resting between bloody bouts. There was no way I was going to be his or anyone's punchbag over this. I let him have it.

'How about we talk about you for a change, what you and Eddie did, huh?'

'That was a long time ago. So I took the money, so fucking what?'

'You killed someone too. Remember?'

181

He couldn't look at me. He leaned on the bed and stared to one side. 'That was an accident.'

'That was an accident. But I'm talking about now.'

'You're talking shit, I ain't done nothing now,' he said.

'OK, what did Eddie say to her? I call him, he calls her – and don't tell me he didn't – then, hey presto, she wires into the machine. If she was on the edge, it looks like she was pushed.'

Warren wouldn't answer so I gave him some more to think about.

'I've kept quiet about the game so far, Warren, the one you were crawling about in. You know Diane can't write the story. She hasn't got what I've got. I've got printouts and something else she doesn't know, about you and Eddie. Pornoland belongs to you and him, you've known that all along. It fits in with the MT portfolio, doesn't it, leisure, entertainment, gambling. The woman made a mistake to stick me on there, out of some sort of revenge. You knew who I was. You wanted to know why I was there and whether I was on to anything that might lose you both some money. How heavy did Eddie get? Let's talk about that.'

Warren's face was disfigured with contempt. He sat on the bed and leaned back on the raised pillows, his face pale. His words hit me like sticks and stones.

'Get out. I ain't saying nothing to you, never. If I want to tell the papers, I'll fucking tell them myself. You're finished. You're dirt.'

His words hurt me. A real pain knifed at me, somewhere in the middle of my chest. I hadn't come for a fight to the death. I'd wanted his shoulder to cry on and his arms around me. I wanted to tell him how I ached inside, how angry and foolish I felt, how used. I wanted to tell him that the intercourse was nothing, nothing, but that the intrusion was almost too much to bear. I wanted to ask him if it were possible to be relieved to be alive and want to die at the same time. I wanted to ask him if David was right and fear was what I needed to get the juices flowing. I wanted him to say that it wasn't my fault and make love to me. I wanted everything from him, just to stop the raging in me.

But Warren didn't want to know. He didn't believe me. I wasn't a victim. That was plain.

'You get your bag back?' I said. Warren gave me a so-what look.

'Your passport. Says you're married.'

I got the same look.

'Good luck to her,' I said.

David had a dual part to play at the inquest: that of an expert witness and that of the bereaved. There was no noticeable difference in either delivery. I could tell that the coroner and the shabby collection of coughing reporters, policemen – including a rather shell-shocked Robert Falk – forensic and psychiatric experts thought he was a cold fish, just as they thought that I was a tart.

David explained the aim of the project and the workings of the hardware and software as simply as he could. The coroner, a dapper solicitor from the district and not unused to the gadgets and gizmos that emanated from the surrounding area known as Silicon Fen, bore a look of appalled confusion throughout. He seemed not to comprehend that any computer software could have a strangulation option, and who could blame him? David didn't make a show of doing so, but he further intrigued and titillated the gathering by admitting that he had created this virtual world for his wife and that it included, among others, virtual images of himself and his mistress. At this point, everyone in the stuffy little room, except David, looked at me. My cheeks flared red and my neck burned hotly. I felt guilty as hell, and looked it.

There was no question but that this was a single-user

catastrophe, he said, and a worried-looking engineer from Virtech agreed, since no other peripheral, and no one else's suit, was linked in at the same time. The police experts were of the same opinion. In short, the computer and Julie Jones had been alone together.

It was when he began to describe her that I wondered how many of her psychological clothes he'd borrowed, or shared. Julie, David said, had been slightly autistic as a child. There was a doctor's letter to substantiate this, which the coroner discreetly referred to. David explained that his wife found it difficult to show or receive affection and it had put a strain on an otherwise happy marriage. He admitted that he had had affairs in the past, but that his wife had tolerated them because they were, otherwise, very compatible. No one in the room registered any astonishment at this admission. It was, after all, a very traditional marital situation, one imbued with true Victorian values.

The coroner tentatively asked David if he knew why she would have chosen the strangulation option available on the machine.

'To experience power, and helplessness. She wanted to control her own helplessness. She was, frankly, very excited by it. We were told it was not unusual. For example, many women have rape fantasies. But fantasy figures can be controlled. No woman wants to be attacked by a real live rapist.'

'Quite so, Dr Jones, so did your wife ever, em, have this, strangulation, experience in reality, in real life, with another human being?' the coroner asked.

'Possibly,' David replied, 'but not with me.'

It was a scandal, but not a complete one because, of the three people who knew what David Jones was really about, one was dead, one was a psychiatrist, who may or may not have existed, and the other had been his alibi for the night in question.

I explained to the inquest that, for a short time, David Jones had been my lover but that once I had found out that he was married, I had tried to end the relationship. I explained that David Jones was waiting for me when I arrived back from the pub. I admitted that I had had too much to drink and that I had run away from him and struck my head. After that, I said, I couldn't remember much else. I didn't bother with any more details because I didn't have the courage to. I couldn't tell them, couldn't tell an open court, couldn't explain it all. And, if I told them what he had said to me the morning after she had died, I'd have to.

The coroner nodded and noted that I'd been the first to report the story of Julie's death in a national newspaper. I looked over at Robert Falk but he was watching David.

People who worked with her spoke, but no friends. A pony-tailed Scotsman from Babylon Software described her as 'a genius with concepts, really brilliant' but not a mixer, a bit too 'cold and superior' for most, but he got on all right with her. She had a sense of humour, he said, and a ferocious temper. He recalled how she raged if a project she had worked on was criticized in any way, within Babylon, or subsequently, by the press. No matter how small or constructive the criticism, she took it badly and she never forgot the person she supposed had slighted her. That's why she worked freelance, he said, it suited everyone better.

David's secretary at Virtech said that she felt that sometimes Julie could be rather brisk – 'the boss's wife' – but she was always fair. She'd never heard the couple row. They always treated each other with respect, she said. Kid gloves, more like, I said to myself as I jotted down notes like the rest of the hacks.

One extra fact that the secretary gave confirmed what I had suspected. Julie had received a telephone call from one of her husband's partners in America which had made her terribly angry. A technician at Virtech said that the couple had had a meeting and that David had left shortly afterwards. He had heard no angry exchanges.

The profile of Julie Jones created at the inquest went some way to explaining why she should have indulged herself on the virtual reality machine, but not why anyone would have wanted her dead, or if she herself had wanted to die. Those who knew her described a busy, ambitious, highly intelligent professional person with high standards. Any contribution I might have made with tales of snuff games in Pornoland would have seemed like the mouthing of a jealous mind.

No one asked me what David liked to do to me and I didn't volunteer. I couldn't let them find out about it all, let them agree that I'd asked for it. I duly reported the open verdict for my tabloid. *Technology Week* got it from Diane. Max was OK about it but he said I owed him the MT Industries connection. I felt like telling him who was involved. He'd remember then, remember how he'd had to scrap my story all those years ago because someone bigger had kicked his ass.

My tabloid didn't stop at the story. It ran an editorial, boiling with righteous rage, and who was to say it was wrong? The machine, it said, provided dirty trips for perverts, misrepresented innocent people, i.e. me. It argued that pornography reinforced disgusting sexual behaviour and that Virtech's project was not only dangerous, it was a disgrace. The more serious broadsheets took up the story too, taking the line that while the sensitive, innovative treatment of offenders was laudable, was this the treatment they should have? How proven was it? They were concerned with the potential offered by the machine to ruin reputations, to include people in fantasies who had no wish or desire to be there, i.e. me. Meanwhile, Virtech was being inundated with requests

for treatment and pestered by morally unsound entre-
preneurs, who saw a big market in custom-built porn.
Julie Jones had been a visionary.

The time was ripe to let them have it with the stuff
about the porn game but two things held me back: I
hadn't nailed MT Industries and I didn't like to admit
that my face had turned up elsewhere. To paraphrase,
once is unfortunate, twice is carelessness. I had to think
of the effect this was having on my family too. I got a call
from my parents. They didn't want to see me at all now.
My father thundered outrage down the line. My mother
prised the receiver from his fist to tell me that the whole
business had upset him. It would blow over, she said, and
couldn't I take a holiday? I had upset everybody. In a
state of sanctimonious meltdown, Richard told me to get
out of the house. He relented when Diane told him he
was being ridiculous. The man couldn't make up his own
mind any more.

Robert Falk avoided me at the inquest and whenever I
looked over at his familiar bulk squeezed in at the back
of the musty room his huge face was set as blank as a
blancmange. He waited for me afterwards. I'd come to
the inquest with the tabloid's cameraman in a pool car.
Lots of bulbs went off in my face but I didn't really care.
They took their pictures and rushed off to their cars.
Robert opened the door of his for me.

'Do I have to ask what you think?' I said.

'I think you should have taken that holiday, Mrs
Powers. Lunch?' he said, and put the old leather-
upholstered Jag in gear. We didn't go far, twenty minutes
into the green flat countryside to a village pub. Robert sat
me in a quiet corner while he went to order beer and
food. When he returned, we had to heave the iron table
out a foot to get his bulk in beside me on the paisley-
patterned bench seat. He put the ticket under the ashtray.

'Number twelve. They'll give us a shout,' he said,

lifting the golden draught bitter to his plump Cupid-bow lips.

I took my cigarettes out of my bag.

'I thought you were giving those up,' he said, sucking the froth from his lips.

I lit up, noticing spent matches in the ashtray. 'Now is not the time,' I said. 'Anyway, I thought you were dieting.'

'It's hard,' he said, patting his stomach wistfully.

The food proved why, plump home-made pies with sweet garden peas and thick gravy. We cleared our plates and pushed them away satisfied.

'Why did you go to see Warren?' I said.

'Just had to let him know the form.'

'He said you asked him to . . . go away.'

'I thought it might be by far the best idea, for everyone concerned.'

'For me?'

'For everyone.'

'He said his room had been broken into, his things had been tampered with.'

'Oh, yes? Anything missing?'

I hesitated before I said no and Robert took my hand in his large pudgy fingers.

'Make David Jones pay for what he did, Georgina,' he said, taking a hand away to push the steel frame of his glasses up his nose.

'And what do you think he did, Robert?' I said, looking right at him.

He looked right back, sure of me and himself. 'He raped you, and he killed his wife.'

'The first I'm sure about. The second, I'm not.'

'I am. Why didn't you come to me?'

'What, afterwards . . .?'

'Before . . . He had no right to abuse you.'

'How'd you know? You and Warren have a chat?'

'He said there were things he'd like to do to the man. I advised him against it. The law can handle it but we need witnesses.'

'I'm no witness.'

'You weren't afraid to write half the story.'

'Yeah, well. I can't write about this. I can't even talk about it. Thanks anyway.'

Robert sighed and patted my hand. 'For what?'

'For being on my side, unconditionally.'

'Well, we're friends, aren't we?' he said.

CHAPTER SIXTEEN

It was early on a Friday evening and I'd found a space for myself and a large gin and tonic by the bar in The Crown and Two. The weather was unusually warm for early October, warm enough for most of the punters to be outside in their shirtsleeves crowding the pavements. I wasn't too interested in mixing with the team from the office. True or not, I got the feeling that they only ever thought of one thing when they saw me, so whenever I opened my mouth every word came out like a clenched fist. I couldn't have an easy conversation with anyone any more so, more often than not, I sat by myself. When Diane came in, she saw me straight away, and came to stand beside me.

'Drink?'

'I'm fine, thanks,' I said.

She ordered something light, a lager shandy, and clinked her glass against mine.

'We'd make a great team, y'know,' she said and I grunted into my glass.

'We would,' she said.

'Different talents, eh?' I replied.

'You bet.'

'Diane, you're great looking, and as sharp as paper. You don't need to be on any team. You can get what you want all by yourself.'

'How've you been?' she said.

Fine had to be the answer. It would be a lie but to tell the truth would be like knitting with spaghetti, too difficult and altogether pointless. I hadn't had a straight look or a normal conversation with Richard in weeks. His eyes said, 'I told you so.' He even said it. He said if I had gone to the police in the first place, none of this would have happened. The verdict at the inquest hadn't fooled him. Warren didn't even have to hear it to make up his mind. David could have killed her, probably did, everyone knew that. He could have set the machine and she could have plugged in without checking. But who could prove it beyond a shadow of a doubt? Not me.

'Fine,' I said.

'Mmm. You fine, girl, then you black and I'm white.'

I didn't answer. She was right, but I had to keep it all inside. Diane wasn't going to give up. She looked cheekily at me over the rim of her glass.

'OK. This Eddie Powers. The guy who called Virtech. He a relation or something?'

I laughed, though not much. The girl had a lot of class. I told her who he was and asked how she'd found him.

'He's the guy who called the secretary. He's MT Industries. Virtech's partner. She told me the call was from Las Vegas, gave me the number. It was The Dice Palace. That's where our friend Warren works, isn't it?'

'Has Eddie told you anything?' I said.

'Not yet.'

'Maybe you should get yourself there. Once he sees you, well, I guarantee . . .'

Diane shook her head. Max would never agree to the budget.

'Why don't you drop the story, Diane? The woman's dead. You won't get diddly-squat out of Eddie if his ass is on the line, and as for Warren, he won't tell anyone anything now . . .' I said.

'Virtual sex victim ran porn game? It's too good,

George. I'm surprised at you. With the hassle you've had, I would have thought you'd have wanted to show her up for what she was.'

'And what was that?'

'A class A bitch.'

'She had a right to be. I was making out with her husband.'

'Come on, don't be so hard on yourself. What about the porn?'

'It was smut, so what? Consenting adults and all that.'

'Are you sure? Warren said it got pretty bad.'

'He also said the details got to you. He still around?'

Diane crossed her elegant legs and smoothed her hand all the way down one shin to ring her narrow ankle with her long fingers. I thought of Warren's leg, uncovered, on the bed. Too bad.

'You see that Jones guy at all?' Diane said.

I had to be careful now that she was asking that sort of question. I made a show of shaking the cigarette pack on the bar even though I knew it was empty.

'Look at that. That's it. I'm giving up. As of now, I'm on a health kick. No more ciggies, no more booze, no more . . . sex . . . that's it. From now on this body is a temple,' I said.

'So it is. But, come on, what about him?' she said.

I looked down at myself slouching on the bar stool, ash on my tight black skirt. I looked up at the mirror. My roots were showing and I looked tired. I was thinking aloud when I spoke.

'Ancient ruin, more like.'

'As in classically beautiful?' Diane volunteered.

'As in just plain knackered,' I replied.

'Come on. What about this Jones guy?'

'I don't hear from him.'

'Seriously?'

'Seriously. He doesn't need me, remember?'

'Oh yes, I'm sorry, I forgot.'

It was at that moment that I felt lonely. Just for a moment, because in the next I felt ashamed. I'd thought of him and felt him under my skin. I knew that he would be thinking of me even though I could always be there, predictable and synthetic, less than he wanted, but all that he could get, not blonde, brown and free, but pale, dark and compliant. I should have been relieved that I hadn't heard from him, but I felt incomplete. We had unfinished business to attend to and I wondered how long it would take for him to show.

'Listen,' I said to Diane. 'I'm going to give you a little tip, save you some time digging through MT Industries. Warren and Eddie are partners, don't ask me how come. They own The Dice Palace, they are MT Industries Holdings.'

'Well, well, so Warren owns a slice of the credit company and Virtech?'

'Right.'

Diane leaned on the bar and circled her finger around the rim of her glass. She was thinking. I didn't speak until she did. I fiddled with my blue plastic Zip lighter. It was hard not smoking, maybe I could chew matchsticks instead, break them into pieces.

'You know, he's still hanging on to that security guard line too. Jones didn't know him, I'm sure of that. Did his wife?' she said.

'Neither of them did. Eddie was the front man. She suspected Warren had played the porn game, that much I do know. I don't think she knew anything more until Eddie telephoned her, once he found out that I was sniffing around. She got into big trouble about me. I think it hurt her pride,' I said.

'Was Warren lying about the game?'

'About playing it? No. He played it and lost a lot of money.'

'How come?'

'He just did.'

'So why play a game you, excuse me, virtually own for money? Lose or not. Do you think he was checking it out?'

I dug in my bag for some loose change and hurried to the cigarette machine. There was a five-minute queue. When I got to the front, I slammed the money in and tugged out the packet. That was it. Warren had come here to check up on Eddie. Diane was right. When he'd been playing that game, he hadn't known he owned it. When he lost and got behind the scenes of Julie's machine he found out that MT Industries was involved. He found out how much I was involved too. No wonder I didn't recognize him. Warren was on a white charger.

I felt sick. No surprise that Eddie moved so fast when I had asked him about the game. He didn't want me nosing around, but most of all, he didn't want Warren to be. I walked back to the bar and stared at the unfinished drinks on the counter. Diane wasn't there. In the ashtray, with the butts of my cigarettes, there were three matchsticks, broken and unspent.

I pushed past the drinkers on the pavement looking desperately for Diane. I couldn't see anyone I knew on this side. No one to ask if they'd seen her pass by and if she was with someone. I heard the diesel engine of the cab first and then saw it drive by. Two heads, one black, one fair, talking together, and then his face turning to look out of the window at me. I shouted, 'Wait!' loudly enough for people to stare, but the cab drove off and my hand stayed up waving for another. I was lucky.

'You know what to do,' I said, as the cabbie rolled back the dividing glass and leaned back to hear.

'Follow that cab?' he said.

'Yes . . . Wait a minute.'

I threw open the door again and ran past three men

laughing on the corner. There was a bottle on a window sill next to some dirty glasses. I grabbed it and ran back to the cab.

'I collect labels,' I said to the cabbie.

'If you haven't got Guinness, what have you got, love?' he said and clicked the handle of my door shut.

The evening traffic was heavy as we drove northwards. We lost sight of the cab in front once or twice but my cabbie seemed to be on autopilot.

'Where's he going?' I called through the glass.

'King's Cross, love. Must have a train to catch.'

People who travel to Cambridge depart from King's Cross, a wide modern station built on a junction where the Gray's Inn, Pentonville and Caledonian Roads converge on King's Cross. Commuters criss-cross over the square concourse within its glass doors past prostitutes, patient for passing trade. I couldn't believe that Diane would go to Cambridge at this time of night with David Jones, but there they were, in front of me, hurrying through the doors that led into the station as my cab pulled briskly into the rank. I paid up, tipped heavily and followed. First, I checked the boards and the screens. The Cambridge train was due to leave in thirty minutes. Plenty of time. They'd be in the busy bar, or buying their tickets. I'd have to get one too. I looked around for the sign, one way and then another, and there he was. Watching me, watching me think and move and sweat. I walked straight up to him.

'Where's Diane?'

'In the car.'

'What are you doing?'

'Waiting for you. I saw you following. She seemed quite glad. I don't think she wants to travel with me on her own.'

'What's this all about, David?'

'It's about the game Julie ran and your black friend financed. I found the machine. There's a lot of interesting material on it. Even I am on it.'

'That what you told Diane?'

'That's what she wanted to hear. I decided she deserved a scoop.'

'What about a scoop for me, David?'

'I've already given you one. Why don't you use it?'

I watched his back retreating and called out his name. He didn't answer. He carried on, walking out of the doors past the taxi rank, where we had arrived minutes before, and into a side road by St Pancras station. It was badly lit and lined with old brick railway arches that housed little workshops and warehouses, busy during the day but all shuttered up for the night.

As I caught up with him, I half shouted: 'Where's the car?'

He turned and took me firmly by the arm. I pulled away and stopped dead. He began walking backwards and beckoning.

'Come on,' he said, turning his back to me once again.

I didn't move until, twenty feet from me, he disappeared from sight behind a high-sided van, the last of a whole line parked there for the night. I suspected that he was crossing the road but I had to be cautious. I walked slowly towards the back of the van. The dark metal-walled space between it and a large lorry parked behind it was empty. I stepped out slowly into the road, looking left and right. I couldn't see the car, I couldn't see him, or Diane.

They say fear has its own special odour. I was afraid all right, but I could only smell the diesel-soaked road and the lingering aroma of warm engines and cooling tyres. The traffic along the Euston Road rumbled in the distance but it was quiet as a prayer where I stood, save for the odd tick of a settling engine, like rosary beads

196

flicking slowly over fingers. I could feel arteries of blood pulsing behind my ears. My shoulders dropped and my hands fell to my hips. He'd fooled me, left me there and gone back for her. The car was somewhere else. I stepped back, turned around and he was there on the pavement, like a trick of the light, his eyes shadowed by the lenses of his spectacles.

'There you are,' he said.

'Come on, David. Not now,' I said.

'Oh yes, now, Georgina.'

'Please.'

'Are you afraid, Georgina?' he said.

'No,' I lied.

'I know you are.'

'No, I'm not. Too much of a good thing at the wrong time can put you off. You know how it is.'

'What if I said I could kill you here and who would know?'

'Diane would.'

'She doesn't know you're here. She thinks I'm going to my car to get something for her. Something for her to play with before she goes to bed. I just wanted to get you here. Make you afraid like you really want to be.'

I ducked quickly behind the van and started to run down the road on the outside of the vehicles. I had no speed. My lungs had been shrunk by too many cigarettes, and booze did not convert into the sort of energy I needed to beat a regular tennis player in a hundred-yard dash. He cut me off by a small Ford Escort, catching me in his arms. Through wheezes and gasps, I tried to reason with him with the sort of banter I'd learned he could accept.

'OK, OK. So there's just you and me. What's your beef? You don't fancy me any more, surely? Look at me. I look like Brigitte Nilsen, shorter maybe, pre-vulcanized, of course, but nevertheless . . .'

'I'm bored, Georgina.'

'You've got the machine.'

'I'm bored by the machine.'

'And me. You're bored by me.'

'No, never. You're alive. Death has real meaning to you.'

'But you can control that machine . . .'

'. . . Don't try taking me for a fool.'

'I'm not. I don't.'

'I don't have it any more. I don't have anything. Didn't your black man tell you? He's cut off my head, Georgina, clean as a whistle.'

'I don't get it,' I said, hurting from the pressure of his fingers gripping my arms and a cold deepening well of disquiet in my stomach.

'My partner. Your friend. My wife's revenge on me. He closed me down. See how dangerous proximity is? I said, didn't I? I said she was dangerous, bringing him in with subterfuge and stealth, to humiliate me. She had her revenge. I had mine.'

'She didn't know about him. It was just business, David.'

'She brought them in and now there's no project. No project. No machine. No machine, no money, no nothing.'

'Did you kill her, David?'

'She should have checked but I knew she never did. I wanted her then, but I was with you, thinking about her. Funny, isn't it? How things end.'

We stood together, me staring into his face, trying to work out the best exit lines. I didn't have long. He was tired of waiting.

'OK,' I said. 'Let's do it. You're right. I've missed you. Do something really special this time. I want to be afraid.'

'How much?'

'You know how much. I didn't tell them, did I?'

He released his grip and stood back with a little smile, nothing that would give me much hope.

'Have a cigarette. I want to see you take the smoke, right in through your mouth, right down here,' he said, his fingers pushing at my breasts.

I still had my bag. Its strap was cutting into my shoulder. I lifted up the flap and reached down inside for the pack I'd bought from the machine. With shaking fingers, I blessed my weak willpower and ripped the cellophane away. He had something in his hand, a small box. Matches. His fingers moved quickly and a spitting flame caught the trail of transparent viscose wrapping. It bloomed with heat as it fell burning away from my hand. I stuck a cigarette in my mouth and waited. His fingers snapped the spent match and he delivered another, holding it ablaze three inches from my face. I inhaled and blew out the hot flame with a quick blast of smoke.

'Kiss me, Georgina,' he said, removing his glasses and narrowing his eyes. One hand quickly gathered my T-shirt into a fist of material and swung me to one side so that my back slammed into the low van. He wasn't expecting an answer, a yes or no. His face came towards me, mouth half open, eyes wide open, until, a split second before his lips pressed over mine, his lids closed, like any dreaming lover, shutting out everything but the touch and smell of skin and the internal workings of his own mind. I allowed myself no such luxury. I stuck the red-hot tip of my cigarette into the back of his neck and brought my knee up into his hard groin. He thudded to his knees with a grunt, his head level with my hips. I rammed my hand into my bag again and felt for the bottle. It was hard and cool, still a little beer in it. He was sighing with pain now, trying to lift his head. I didn't want him to get up because I was still here, watching him. The bottle was in my hand, I had it by the neck. He was on his knees and it was my only chance. I hit him, once, twice, three times, until the bottle broke and the groaning stopped. I pushed his body with my foot and stepped over him. First I walked and then I ran, and what I lacked in muscularity, I made up for in overproduction of adrenalin. I reached the station doors as Diane walked out.

'Where the hell is he?' she said.

'Never mind, move, move,' I said, pushing her towards the rank and staring past it to the corner of the road.

'He said he had stuff from her machine.'

'Jesus, Diane, get in the cab. You want that fucking story, I'll give it to you.'

'It's a deal . . . Hey, not so rough,' she said as I bundled over her into the back of the cab.

CHAPTER SEVENTEEN

Diane sat with me on her sofa until I said: 'I think I killed him.'

She stayed with me, sitting in silence at the edge of her seat, her arm over my shoulder.

'With a beer bottle. I hit him with a beer bottle. He went for me, so I hit him, hit him, hit him.'

'I'll get you a drink,' she said, walking barefoot across the polished floorboards into the kitchen area.

I thought I was getting a brandy but she began filling the kettle with water. I looked around and up at the high ornate ceilings of the blush pink room and shivered. The slide from the steep gradient high I'd felt all the way home had begun. The lead-weighted doubts were settling in. I couldn't stop shivering. I knew that he wasn't going to kill me. To him I was re-usable, he couldn't kill me. It would have been such a waste. He was just going to hurt me a little, and then a lot, and then he would want repayment for the pleasure he thought he had given. I paid him back all right. That's what I did, I paid him back. He couldn't just take me. I paid him back.

The scrape of a coffee cup on wood startled me and then Diane's warm dark arms were around my shoulders again, preventing me from rocking back and forth.

'I'll call a doctor. You need a doctor, George, really you do.'

'Call the police,' I said. 'No, call Robert Falk, two

numbers in my bag, home and work.'

'Who's he?'

'He's a friend, a real friend. Call him first, he'll know what to do.'

He wasn't in, but I made Diane call every half-hour for two hours, and when she got through he came straight away. I waited for him as a dog, tortured by the promise of return, waits outside a shop for his master. I didn't cry when I saw him, just smiled desperately and jabbered an incoherent story to him, at speed. He did the best thing, he put his great big overweight arms around my shuddering body and held me close. He let me sob over his shirt and blow my nose into his large, clean, blue handkerchief before instructing Diane to ring for a doctor.

I couldn't stop talking and I couldn't stop shaking. I pressed the dying end of one cigarette into the fresh tip of another and rambled out the story, backwards from the time when I hit the back of David's skull with a bottle. Hit it and hit it. I didn't hear the knock on the door, nor feel the sharp needle in my arm, nor turn to the soft click of the bedroom door shutting. But I saw a familiar holdall in the corner of the room, and just before I closed my eyes, I remembered Warren.

Late in the afternoon, the following day, Robert Falk and a young solicitor sat with me as I dictated my monotonous statement to a detective sergeant in a blank-walled police interview room. They had found David's body, slumped by the Ford Escort van, right where I said it would be, where I had left him. He had a fractured skull, bruising and bad lacerations but the post-mortem showed it was the bullet that had made the hole in his temple that had killed him. Diane got the story for the Sunday papers, and a by-line. I had a reprieve.

Diane shoved her hand into the folds of her large Burberry check umbrella.

'Right time to go to a health farm, I can tell you,' she said.

The heavy rain was coming down in hard cold drops as we walked down Old Compton Street. Dirty water left muddy spots on our black leggings and the tail-lights of the bumper to bumper cars reflected bleary red in the oily puddles by the kerb.

My hand on her back guided Diane across the busy road as she wrestled with the umbrella, obstinately fixed shut. Warren had discharged himself from hospital and moved into Diane's for a few days, on her invitation, just to see how he coped, before moving out to a hotel in Mayfair. Richard hadn't liked it and had said so, but I got the feeling he was on the way out now that Diane was on the way up.

We stood outside a busy sweet-smelling patisserie and Diane's umbrella shot open, taking the skin from her middle finger.

'You guys ought to apologize to each other,' she said, sucking on the tweaked skin.

'I just want to ask him something. I've got nothing to apologize for, Diane.'

She passed me the umbrella to hold above our heads as she buttoned up the wide collar of her long black PVC mac.

'Look, he tried to be a good friend but don't blame him for wanting more. He thought you had thrown everything you may have had together in one drunken night. He thought you were backing up the Jones guy. He loves you. Really,' she said, looking out at the weather and scowling. 'Shit, why today of all days?'

'Listen, nothing those guys like better than a wet, shiny, black . . .'

'Pussy?'

'Plastic coat. Good luck.'

I patted her shoulder and she strode away through the

surface water to her big interview and maybe a new job on a Sunday scandal sheet. She'd earned the right, for sure. I watched her turn the corner, gave her the thumbs up, and made my way to Mayfair with the address of the hotel where Warren was staying. I didn't care about the rain.

The hotel was small but elegant, tucked away in a narrow street behind a discreet, black door with a snarling, brass cat's head for a knocker. A slightly built man in an elegant double-breasted suit phoned the room number and said that Mr Graham was in his room and that I could go up. I took the lift to the second floor and walked a short way down a blue-carpeted corridor, whose walls were lined with original watercolours of hopelessly idealized rural views of an England that never knew a hypermarket or a three-lane bypass.

I knocked and Warren's familiar voice said, 'Come in.'

He was lying on a double bed, resting his back on two large, soft pillows, his arms tucked behind his head. He was wearing just a pair of jeans and watching a children's television programme. It reminded me of another time, in another hotel room, but now, instead of sandalwood, there was a ripe smell of cannabis.

'You look a lot better,' I said.

Warren looked up and then back at the screen.

'Thanks. Take off your coat, you're dripping all over the nice man's carpet.'

I unbuttoned my coat but kept it on. It was warm in the room, but I wasn't intending on staying long.

'When are you leaving?' I said.

'I got a flight tonight. You're lucky to catch me.'

'I thought I'd save myself a transatlantic call.'

'Oh yeah?'

'I just want to ask you one thing and then I don't ever want to speak to you again.'

His eyes blinked as he watched the programme's credits scroll up. He didn't turn his head.

'Diane said I should apologize to you,' he said.

'You know what for?'

'She said I didn't understand how bad it was.'

'She said I should apologize to you too.'

'You know what for?'

'Haven't a clue.'

He picked up the TV controller and flipped through a few channels before settling on some shots of white water canoeing. He put the controller on the bed and reached for a burning ashtray on his bedside table.

'Want some blow?' he said.

'Thanks all the same.'

'Used to like the stuff as I remember.'

'Used to like a lot of things.'

Warren looked across at me with interest. The ashtray balanced on his lean brown stomach, which was pulled in naturally so that it left the top of his belted jeans a little loose around the hips. His smooth chest was shadowed with the stains of old bruises and his face bore a large scab but, otherwise, he'd healed up well. He took a toke and stared back at the television before starting to laugh.

'Used to like me, yeah? Oh baby, baby, baby.'

'The weapon that went missing. You made a point of telling me. What was it?' I said.

'A Smith and Wesson .38 two-inch. Look at that fucking guy go.'

'You ever get it back?'

'Nah.'

'You report it missing?'

'Nah.'

'A Smith and Wesson .38, two-inch barrel?'

'That's the one. Weighs less than a pound, didn't spoil the line of me strides. Shouldn't worry about it. I can get another in Vegas. No probs.'

205

'They dug a bullet from a Smith and Wesson, two-inch barrel, out of David Jones's head.'

'No shit? Leaves four in the barrel. I'd have emptied it into the sicko.'

'You didn't do it?'

'I told you. Someone nicked it from my room. Sure as hell don't want the thing back now.'

'You didn't make that story up then? Just in case anyone asked me?'

'No.'

'Who took it?'

'Whoever was watching me, I suppose. Thought maybe I'd come back for trouble. Wanted to avoid any bother.'

'Who?'

'Aw, be nice, Georgie. I came all the way over here with such good intentions.'

'I know,' I said. His shoulders seemed to slump with the gentler tone in my voice. He picked the ashtray off his belly and put it back on the table.

'C'm here,' he said, beckoning. 'C'm here. C'm here. Come on, please.'

I walked over and stood by the side of the bed. My coat flapped open and he took a long look at where my dark leggings disappeared into my short, black skirt. His hand tugged at my coat, pulling me down on to the bed. I didn't pull away. I rested on one knee and let him roll me over on my back so that my head lay in the crook of his elbow. He smiled down at me, his greenish eyes a little foggy-looking and his teeth white and even.

'The gun was mine but Smith and Wesson's standard police issue, it's a familiar piece, know what I mean?'

I thought maybe I did. Warren licked his dry lips and the spit glistened like gloss. He smelled nice, like herbal soap. In all this time, he hadn't changed the brand, it hadn't gone upmarket with his vests and underwear. His face was close to mine as he spoke, his finger drawing round the shape of my lips.

'My money's on your fat friend, the cop who's so straight you could draw lines with him. Did us all a favour, for a change. Tell me, did you mean all that stuff you told me?' he said.

'When?'

'C'mon, you know when.'

I didn't answer and his face got closer and closer until our mouths connected. At first, I lay there passive and quiet as a cellophane-wrapped doll, made him work at it until he started to give up, then I gave him something to remember me by. I kissed him good and hard, and good and soft, in turns, biting at his lips and tongue until his hand moved eagerly over my breast and under my skirt. That's when I pushed him gently away. His eyes were all but question marks as I got off the bed and straightened my coat.

'I think I've always wanted to do that,' I said.

'You have? Well, come back down here, what are you doin'?'

'I've done it now.'

'And that's it?'

'That's it.'

'Why?'

'I don't go with married men.'

I turned, opened the door and walked quickly back down the corridor. Warren jumped up and was by the door before I got to the lifts. He shouted at me as I punched the descend button.

'You had us all on a string, didncha? That poor dead bastard and the fat cop. Well, I ain't no more. You hear me? You hear me? I ain't no more. I got you when and how I want, got that? I got that machine, bought it, you hear? Bought it with fucking money.'

The lift doors opened with a whisper and I got in and

shoved the buttons inside about three times in the hope that they'd hurry along and close right away. I stood with my back against the soft, quilted velveteen and closed my eyes. I could still hear his voice screaming as the doors hissed shut.

The waiter took away the brightly stained dishes and the hot plate as Robert Falk poured clear blossom-coloured tea into the little china cup by my hand.

'I must say you look marvellous, Mrs Powers, tanned, fit, relaxed,' he said.

'Thank you. It was expensive, but worth it,' I said, dipping my fingers in the lemon bowl. 'But who was counting the pennies anyway? I barely took out a year's interest.'

'Amazing, isn't it? The overtime I'd have had to do . . . Tell me, is that your natural colour now?' he said, lifting the steaming tea to his moist lips.

I brushed my fingers through the short, dark urchin cut and said, 'Who knows?'

He liked that. His big sandy head shook with laughter until the waiter interrupted us with a plate of hot banana fritters and some honey. Robert took my dish and scooped three sticky portions on to it.

'Good food, eh? Not like that health farm,' he said, tucking into his dessert when he was sure I had started on mine.

'Gawd, those lonely strips of chicken . . .'

'Well, as you can see, I've never rated health farms myself.'

'It was all right for a couple of days but I think Bali was better,' I said.

He looked over his fork and his eyes glinted, the single mole on his well-covered cheekbone moving up with a growing smile.

'Yes, it was, wasn't it? You can see the picture, read

the book, but the real thing is hard to beat, isn't it, Mrs Powers?' he said, licking his lips.

All Orion/Phoenix titles are available at your local bookshop or from the following address:

Mail Order Department
Littlehampton Book Services
FREEPOST BR535
Worthing, West Sussex, BN13 3BR
telephone 01903 828503, *facsimile* 01903 828802
e-mail MailOrders@lbsltd.co.uk
(Please ensure that you include full postal address details)

Payment can be made either by credit/debit card (Visa, Mastercard, Access and Switch accepted) or by sending a £ Sterling cheque or postal order made payable to *Littlehampton Book Services*.
DO NOT SEND CASH OR CURRENCY

Please add the following to cover postage and packing

UK and BFPO:
£1.50 for the first book, and 50p for each additional book to a maximum of £3.50

Overseas and Eire:
£2.50 for the first book plus £1.00 for the second book and 50p for each additional book ordered

---

BLOCK CAPITALS PLEASE

name of cardholder ....

address of cardholder ....

....

....

....

postcode ....

delivery address
(*if different from cardholder*)

....

....

....

postcode ....

☐ I enclose my remittance for £ ....

☐ please debit my Mastercard/Visa/Access/Switch (delete as appropriate)

card number

expiry date

Switch issue no.

signature ....

prices and availability are subject to change without notice